Lady Maggie's Challenge

The Buckingham Sisters, Volume 1

Robyn C Rye

Published by robyncrye, 2023.

This is a work of fiction. Similarities to real people, places, or events are entirely coincidental.

LADY MAGGIE'S CHALLENGE

First edition. July 10, 2023.

ISBN: 979-8223138181

Written by Robyn C Rye.

Also by Robyn C Rye

Farnsworth Sisters
Marrying a Rogue
Rescuing Hannah

The Buckingham Sisters
Lady Maggie's Challenge
Layla's Unwanted Husband

The Evans Family
Sometimes Love is not Enough
Still the One
Moving Forward

Standalone
One More Chance
Lady Jayne's Reputation
Third Time's the Charm
Can't Stop Loving You

The Marriage Scam
An Unlikely Match
Searching For You
The Unexpected Suitor
The Lady and the Duke
Starting Over
An Unforgettable Stranger
The Duke's Revenge
The Temporary Wife
Against The Odds
Betrayed
No Good Turn Goes Unpunished
Lady Eloise's Soldier
Lillian's Forbidden Beau
Remember Me
Always Second Best
When One Door Closes
Coming Home to You
Chasing Shadows
Fool Me Once
Deserting Lady Audrey
My Unlikely Saviour
Lies and Deception
A New Beginning
Julia's Second Chance
The Hidden Enemy
The Maiden's Redemption
Miss Elizabeth's Season

Author's message

I am an Australian author, so the spelling of some words may differ from that used in American English.

Thank you for joining me in telling the story of Maggie and Theo. I hope you liked their story as much as I enjoyed recounting it.

If you enjoyed the book and have a moment to spare, I would appreciate a brief review on the page or site where you purchased the book. Reviews from readers like you make a massive difference in helping new readers find stories like Lady Maggie's Challenge. Your help in spreading the word is appreciated.

Thank you!

robyncrye.author@gmail.com

Chapter One

"Maggie, hurry up, or we will be unfashionably late."

"I can't get this bow to sit right. I won't let everyone laugh at me because my bow enters the room before me."

Layla frowned at the bow in question, and with deft fingers, she untied it and redid it so it lay flat.

"There, now are you ready?"

Maggie didn't think now was the right time to tell her sister that she was so nervous about their entry into society that she feared she might be sick. So many things could go wrong, and a shameful entry into society would doom the debutante forever. When the girls descended the stairs, they found their Mother pacing in the foyer.

"At last! The next time we receive an invitation to an event, I will send you two so you can begin dressing immediately after lunch. Come along; we daren't be much later, or Lady Strickland will be annoyed."

The carriage ride to their destination was primarily silent as the girls contemplated their first social event, and Lady Buckingham silently prayed that nothing should go wrong. Years of tutoring and instruction in how a lady presented herself to the ton would come to naught if either of the girls made a faux pas. Lady Buckingham fussed with the girls' dresses as their carriage moved to the side of the driveway beside numerous other vehicles. Even though she dismissed Maggie's nerves, she was anxious for the night to go well.

The mansion's entry hall was jaw-droppingly large and ornate, and Lady Buckingham frowned at Maggie as she gaped at the splendour.

As they moved from the entry hall into the ballroom, the reception line was long, and before the guests could enter, they had to greet their hosts and wait for the butler to announce them. Maggie had practised her curtsy before the mirror before leaving tonight, but feared she might trip and make a fool of herself. When the butler announced their group, and it was their turn to greet the host, Maggie's fears were unfounded as she executed a faultless curtsy. The press of bodies in the ballroom heated the room, and the mixture of perfumes and colognes made the air oppressive. Lady Buckingham moved through the crowd, looking for friends and acquaintances to introduce to her daughters and fill in the girls' dance cards.

While Maggie loved to dance, it didn't take long to categorise the men she danced with; they were either silent, blowhards, or condescending. Why did men think the debutantes could discuss nothing more bothersome than their new bonnets or the ribbons for their hair? Even though she hadn't danced with one man who sparked her interest, the season had just started, and there were men out in the world she hadn't met. As she danced, it became apparent that some girls stood along one wall, and no man approached to dance with them. What was wrong with these debutantes? She vowed to ask her Mother when they left.

When the bandmaster announced the supper waltz, Maggie and Layla watched as elegant men whirled around their partners. Debutantes couldn't dance the waltz until the matrons, who ruled on everything from inappropriate dresses to inappropriate behaviour, gave permission. Debutantes attending their first event were not permitted to waltz, but neither Maggie nor Layla felt disappointed. In time, they would gain approval to dance this most daring of dances.

Hustled on by their Mother, Maggie and Layla passed the dance floor and walked towards the supper room. Maggie grinned; by not waltzing, the debutantes would have the best access to the premier tables and unlimited food. Maggie's thoughts regarding the tables were accurate, but she looked at the morsels of food on her plate and inwardly groaned. She was famished. Her nerves before they arrived had meant that she only had a cup of tea before they left, and now she had to pretend to be a lady and eat barely anything. Why was it all right for the men to load their plates when the ladies had to eat like scarecrows? Maggie hoped her next partner would not have to listen to her grumbly stomach.

As the night wore on, Maggie began to feel tired and longed for a quiet place to rest, but with her dance card filled, she had no opportunity to sit. When her newest partner approached., Maggie pasted on her best smile, and as her partner held out his hand, Maggie placed her hand on his arm as he led her to the dance floor.

"Lady Margaret, I must tell you that even though I wanted to dance with you, I am not looking for a wife. My brother is the Duke of Windslow, and I am the spare, so should the need ever arise where I became the Duke, I would look to do my duty then."

"Well, Lord Reinholt, I am not looking to marry the first man who shows an interest. I have a full season to meet prospective suitors and intend to enjoy myself."

Lord Reinholt smiled at Maggie.

"Miss Margaret, maybe we can enjoy ourselves together without ruining our reputations or breaking hearts. What say you?"

Maggie gave Lord Reinholt a genuine smile. "I think your suggestion is splendid."

For the remainder of the dance, Maggie and Lord Reinholt chatted, and she felt relaxed for the first time tonight. There was no pressure or need to pretend she was demure and shy to capture a gentleman's interest. When Lord Reinholt delivered her to her Mother, Maggie smiled at the man as he took his leave.

Lady Buckingham escorted her daughters to the entry, waiting for their driver to arrive with their coach. She frowned as she recalled the familiarity between her daughter and the man who had danced with her last. If her memory served her well, the man was a second son with no prospects. Maggie should not waste her time with the man, whether he was a Lord or not. When they returned home, she would advise Maggie to dissuade the man. While she intended to speak to her daughter about her last dance partner, she knew the girls were tired, and if she made any suggestions now, they would forget them by morning.

Chapter Two

When Maggie arose, the sun was high in the sky, and she shuddered to think how much of the morning she had wasted. With the assistance of her maid, Maggie dressed in a flowery day dress that would look well enough should the family have any callers. Their Father, Henry Buckingham, quizzed them about their night out. Layla gushed about the finery worn by the ladies and the gentlemen's attire. While Maggie had reservations about the ostentatious display of wealth, considering so many people had little enough to provide for their families, the question of the wallflowers was foremost in her mind.

"While we danced, about five or six debutantes sat in chairs along the wall. No gentleman approached them for a dance, which means they might as well have saved themselves the effort of dressing up. I checked for disfigurements, but there were none I could see, and most girls were attractive enough, so why are they ignored?"

Lady Buckingham tutted. "Those debutantes are girls with no dowries and faint connections to the aristocracy."

Maggie pursed her lips. "So, while a drunken gambler looking to fill his coffers is acceptable enough to court debutantes, perfectly respectable ladies are shunned because they don't have enough money. That is disgusting."

Lord Buckingham nodded. "You're right, Maggie, but that is how the ton has always worked, which is why fathers investigate prospective suitors if the men arrive at the door."

"Speaking of which, Maggie, you need to dissuade Lord Reinholt. He is a second son with no prospects."

"Lord Reinholt and I had a most interesting discussion during our dance. He told me he is the second son, but he is not looking for a wife. I have the entire season to find my prospective husband, so neither of us will ruin our reputations by dancing together, and when I find a suitor, neither of us will have a broken heart. The man is an amusing companion, so that no harm will occur."

"If he continues to dance with you, other gentlemen might assume you have an understanding. I can see no good coming from you dancing and keeping company with the man."

"Let me get this straight. If another gentleman asks to dance twice and spends time chatting, that would be acceptable, but if Lord Reinholt does, it gives the wrong idea. The ways of the ton confuse me; the rules seem convoluted and tedious."

Layla grimaced, her face conveying concern.

"Maggie, don't mess it up for me because you are crusading to make the world fairer. If you can't adhere to the rules, it might be best to separate when we arrive so that people don't assume I am as radical as you."

"Piffle! I am not radical. Just because you were impressed with the glitz and glitter doesn't mean I can't have a different view. I won't share my disappointment at the system's unfairness with anyone else, but why do I have to pretend in my home with my family?"

"That's enough, girls. It must be time to move to the parlour in case we have callers."

Three posies sat in vases along the mantlepiece when they reached the parlour. Maggie assumed they were for her sister because she didn't think she had gendered the interest of any of her dance partners, so it shocked her to discover two of the floral arrangements were for her. The worrying thing about the arrival of the posies was that it generally meant the men would call during the morning session, and she didn't remember either of them. She couldn't sit here and pretend to know the men, so she gave herself an advantage by seeking the butler's help.

"Cummings, if we have any gentlemen callers, will you say their names loudly and clearly? I have two posies from men I don't remember, and I can't imagine anything worse than having them visit while I still can't remember their titles or names."

Maggie watched as the corners of the stalwart butler twitched, and then he said, "Certainly, Miss Maggie."

Maggie grinned. "You are a peach, Cummings."

She could have sworn the butler blushed, but as he turned to face the door, she wasn't sure.

Lady Buckingham and her daughters sat in the parlour, chatting and waiting. When the first knock came, Lydia almost vibrated off her chair with excitement. Maggie paused for the butler's introduction, and when it came, she had no recollection of the man, so when he approached Lydia after greeting the ladies, she sighed with relief. After the first visitor left, a steady stream of gentlemen arrived and departed. When the hour for visiting passed, Maggie felt relieved that she had not offended any visitors by forgetting names and titles.

Over a fresh pot of tea, Lady Buckingham quizzed the girls regarding their interest in the gentlemen callers. Maggie shook her head when Layla gushed about her callers, and Maggie could imagine that her sister might fall in love at least every month or two. Maggie was concerned that Layla didn't think beyond the courtship and the large wedding. Had she considered whether the men she admired were kind and considerate or stubborn and set in their ways? After the glitz disappears, Layla must live with the man of her choice for the rest of her life. When her Mother quizzed her about her callers, Maggie was less effusive than Layla. While the men conducted themselves politely and courteously, none sparked Maggie's interest. They were all cut from the same cloth, and although this was their first week, she feared that she might have to accept the offer of one of these look-alike men.

Maggie wanted to escape the confines that polite society placed on debutantes. If they were in the country, she would have had a groom saddle her horse so she could spend the afternoon roaming the property. Instead of galloping through the countryside, Maggie asked her sister if she wanted to walk in the park. Her Mother declined, and the girls took a maid and a footman as chaperones. When they arrived at the park, a line of vehicles detained their carriage, and rather than wait in the queue, Maggie and Layla alighted and walked along the footpath to the park.

"Are you enjoying your season so far, Layla?"

"Yes, dancing with someone other than our dancing tutor is exciting. I like looking at the older women's dresses, and I wish debutantes didn't have to wear white or pastel colours."

Maggie nodded her agreement. "What about the men? Now that Mother isn't here, you can tell me. Has someone caught your eye?"

"Not yet. What about you? Are you enjoying our outings, Maggie? Is there a man you favour?"

"Will I sound like a killjoy if I say that the men I have danced with fall into three categories? They are either so quiet and nervous that conversation is impossible, or blowhards talking endlessly about their horses or riches. Why do they have to look like clones of one another?"

"Maggie, it's only our second week. If we persevere for a few more weeks, we could ask Mother to accept invitations from less prominent hostesses, which might introduce us to a different type of man."

"Layla, I like that idea. I'll paste on a smile and pretend to be fascinated by every man who asks for a dance, keeping in mind that we have a plan. Thank goodness for Lord Reinhart; he will keep me amused while I suffer the fools the ton think are worthwhile."

"Didn't Mother tell you to dissuade the man?"

"She did, but he is not serious about wife hunting, and he is amusing. If my beauty and wit strike another man, and my occasional dances with Lord Reinhart deter him, he is not too interested.

Debutantes aren't allowed to refuse a dance, so it's not as if I can tell the man no, and in any case, I don't want to deny him. The hardest part of being his dance partner is trying not to laugh out loud at some of his observations. Imagine the scandal! Lady Margaret Buckingham laughed at the ball; how outrageous."

When the sisters arrived at the park, most people remained in their carriages, waving to acquaintances and ensuring other prominent people saw them. As they reached the end of the path, they turned around to retrace their steps. Even though she and Layla had different views about social events and the ton in general, it was nice to discuss things with her sister without her Mother pushing her ideas and thoughts on the girls.

Chapter Three

As they reached the last week of attending balls held by the leading hostesses, Maggie smiled at her latest dance partner and wished the night away. Besides having to smile prettily at her dance partners and the dowagers who occasionally condescended to speak with a mere debutant, Maggie was tired of the endless rounds of visitors and their social obligations to accompany their Mother on her rounds. Was Lord Reinholt the only interesting man in the entire ton?

Maggie was ready to take the floor when there was a sudden and unprecedented level of conversation. From her viewpoint, near the dance floor, someone important appeared to have arrived. The debutantes surrounding her began to preen and titter to one another, and Maggie was at a loss to discover whose arrival had caused so much excitement.

"Why is everyone so excited by the arrival of one man?" Maggie asked her partner.

Her partner scowled. "Lord Windsor is the richest, most influential landowner in these parts. He has only recently become the Duke of Berwick and is supposed to be looking for a wife."

"Oh, well, I'm sure one of those preening females will catch his eye, and he'll be off the market before you know it."

"Hmm, we can only hope."

When her dance partner returned her to her Mother, it astounded Maggie to see her Mother and sister both preening and giggling like five-year-olds. A man stood with her Mother and Layla, and from behind, he appeared well-built; his custom jacket fit his broad shoulders and tapered to a trim waist. Her Mother saw her approach and urged Maggie to join the group. Once her Mother introduced her to the Duke, the man questioned her about the season and her successes with finding a suitor. Maggie felt that her success or otherwise was not a question she should have to answer to a stranger, but her Mother's glare had her reconsidering. There was something predatory about the man, and Maggie hoped he would move on to the more experienced debutantes and leave them alone. From the glazed expression on her sister's face, Maggie knew that the man's purported wealth and his good looks had captivated Layla. It was with relief that Maggie saw Lord Reinholt making his way towards her for their next dance. The Duke glared at Lord Reinholt as though he was interrupting a meaningful discussion, but Maggie took his arm, and the two headed for the dance floor.

"I see your sister is fascinated by the Duke. Do you share her feelings?"

Maggie shuddered. "There is something predatory about the man, and I fear his chosen wife will not lead a charmed existence. Unfortunately, he is the type of man that Layla and a hundred other girls will pine after. Why do the ton place so much importance on wealth and so little on the character of a person?"

"The answer to your question will remain a mystery because I can't explain their fascination."

As they left the dance floor, Maggie realised that the Duke was still in conversation with her Mother and Layla.

"Have you a partner for the next dance?"

"No, but I can't dance with you, or the old biddies will announce the banns tomorrow."

Maggie laughed. "God forbid. No, I hoped we might take a stroll on the balcony."

"We can do that."

The night air was a pleasant change from the stuffy confines of the ballroom; why hostesses aimed for a crush was a mystery to Maggie, because she hated having to battle through hordes of people to reach the retiring room or the dance floor.

"Why haven't you got a partner for this dance, my Lord?"

"Do we know each other well enough to use our first names in private? I would be honoured if you called me Ben."

Maggie nodded. "Yes, please call me Maggie, but you didn't answer my question."

"I don't have a partner because, although it took a while, the Mothers have realised that I am a second son, so I am unworthy of their precious charges. Is your Mother happy about you dancing with me?"

"No, she told me to dissuade you, but I told her you were one of the few amusing dance partners I encountered, and I had no intention of discouraging you. You told me your Father bought an unentailed property for you as a child, and your finances are in good shape. Why don't you broadcast your financial status, and you might receive more acceptance on the dance floor?"

"Why would I want to entertain women who only want my money?"

"You know, you are in the same boat as the wallflowers. I asked my Father why the ton snubs them, and he said they were girls with small dowries or no dowries. They are all of good birth, but their failure to have fathers with titles and no dowries makes them unlikely to catch the eye of most of the men here. Sometimes, their fathers sell them off to old, lecherous men who suddenly realise they need an heir. The only positive thing is that, with any luck, the old men will die and leave the girls widows with substantial funds."

"I never gave the wallflowers or their situation a thought."

"You know, you could make them feel much better if you danced with a few. I can't imagine how demoralising it is to prepare for a ball and wear your best dress, knowing that all you will do is sit against the wall all night. Explain that you are not looking for a wife but are happy to dance with them if they do not try to trap you into a marriage."

As Ben considered Maggie's suggestion, a man blocked their view of the dance floor and the light. The man standing at the balcony entrance stared down at them.

"I hardly think it is appropriate for you to socialise with Lord Reinholt. You are aware he is a second son with no prospects. The woman who marries him will have a hard life."

Ben and Maggie stood, but when Maggie went to reply, Ben shook his head. Maggie raised her eyebrows but then nodded before speaking.

" Lord Windsor, whom I socialise with, is not your concern. We have only met briefly, and it concerns me that you believe you have the right to tell me what I should or should not do."

"We have just met, but I must warn naive debutantes away from shysters."

Ben glared at the man. "You may be a Duke, but you are offensive. Come, Maggie, I will escort you to your Mother."

"I believe it would be better for me to escort Lady Margaret."

As he spoke, he reached for Maggie's hand. When their hands made contact, she yanked hard, attempting to dislodge the man's hand from hers.

"Let me go, you bully, or I will scream. My reputation might take a hit, but a scandal will shatter yours."

Lord Windsor scowled but released her hand.

"We have not finished, my feisty lass."

As Ben returned her to her Mother, he said,

"You were right about the predatory nature of the man. Does he believe he can have any girl for the taking?' You might need to tread carefully."

Lady Buckingham scowled at Ben as he returned Maggie to her side.

"Lord Windsor was asking after you, and I had to admit I was unsure where you were. You can't go off alone with an unsuitable man. If you intend to have a man compromise you, best find a suitable person."

"Mother, Lord Reinholt, and I were in full view of everyone in the ballroom. I have no idea why that man would ask after me. I have no interest in associating with him."

"We will speak of this later."

Maggie knew her Mother would not relent when a man as socially elevated as a Duke was in the offing.

Chapter Four

Lady Buckingham's instruction that Maggie be agreeable when Lord Windsor called aggravated her. The man was pompous and condescending, but Layla was smitten, and Maggie despaired at her sister's naivety. While the man waxed lyrical about his wealth and accomplishments, Maggie smiled inwardly, seething with anger. He overstayed his time limit, and it had come to Maggie's attention that other gentlemen had stopped calling.

The Duke's presence was annoying, but he became bossy and domineering at a ball or social event. Other gentlemen no longer asked her or Layla to dance, and the other debutantes glared at the Buckingham sisters. The one thing that cheered Maggie was seeing Ben dancing with one of the wallflowers. Throughout the evening, she watched as he charmed each girl, and after dancing with them, he returned them to their friends and chose another girl to dance with. The more popular debutantes and their escorts noticed the attention Ben paid the girls, which prompted some men to place their names on the debutantes' cards and engage them in conversation. Despite her anger at Lord Windsow, Ben was a shining light in the dark of her mood.

The following night, as Maggie, Layla, and Phyllis Buckingham entered the ballroom, Maggie decided she refused to be corralled by Lord Windsor tonight. She wanted to dance and chat with her contemporaries.

"Mother, I see a group of acquaintances near the side door. If I join them, you will be able to see me. Please, may I join them?"

Layla said, "What of Lord Windsor? How will he feel if you are socialising with others instead of being here with us?"

"Layla, you may be fascinated with the man; I am not. Have you noticed that since he has monopolised our time, other men no longer ask us to dance? If he is so inclined, he can only have one of us, which won't be me. I need to mix with my friends and chat with other men who might be suitable candidates for a relationship."

When Maggie joined her group of friends, her shoulders relaxed, and she genuinely smiled. There were no prospective suitors amongst this group, but several single men and four ladies she had chatted with before were there, and her Mother had no way of knowing that Maggie was not considering one of the men. A surprised look crossed the faces of the people facing her, and Maggie looked over her shoulder to see what had alarmed her friends. She groaned when she saw Lord Windsor approaching.

"Lady Margaret, your Mother requires your presence immediately. She sent me to escort you to her."

Maggie looked to where her Mother stood, deep in conversation with Lady Spencer. Not once did she look towards Maggie, so the Duke's weak excuse did not add up.

"Thank you for the message, Lord Windsor. I will return shortly."

The man grabbed her arm and said, "She wants you now."

"A glance at my mother disproves your statement, and I do not have to follow your instructions."

The group of revellers whom Maggie had joined looked uncomfortable, and short of scandalising her friends, she had little option but to follow. Lord Windsor lessened his grasp on Maggie's hand without realising that Ben was nearby. With a swift slap, he disconnected Maggie's fingers from the Duke and said, "Lady Maggie, I believe you promised me this dance."

Before the Duke could respond, Ben swirled Maggie onto the dance floor and away from the fuming man. Maggie sagged in Ben's arms; her relief at being freed from the man's punishing grip gladdened her.

"I think, my dear friend, you had better speak to your Father about the man. Because they know I'm your friend, people tend to shy away from talking about you and Layla, but the men are avoiding you because the Duke warned them off."

"Is the man mad? He can only have one of us; it won't be me. Let's forget him for a moment and discuss the wallflowers."

Ben grinned. "You are a genius, my dear. When I began the dance with the wallflowers plan you devised, the girls felt excited and grateful. Nobody expected it to generate interest with other men, but it did, and now, gentlemen are courting two of the wallflowers. I will keep dancing with the debutantes because they are more interesting and honest about their wishes than the stuck-up girls, and if it results in courtships, well, that's terrific."

After her dance with Ben finished, Maggie hid in the retiring room for most of the night. When her Mother found her, she was furious that Maggie was not in the ballroom, but Maggie was adamant that she would not subject herself to Lord Windsor's bullying.

"I can't believe that you think allowing him to corral us in one area of the room where other gentlemen can't talk to us is a good thing. Mother, the man has warned other men away from Layla and me, so when he decides on whichever woman he wants as his wife, the other will be at a disadvantage because the eligible men will have found partners."

"What rubbish. I suppose that near did well, Lord Reinholt told you that rubbish. When we arrive home, I will discuss this with your Father."

"Trust me, Mother; I will discuss this awkward situation with Father. I'm not sure how the Duke has hoodwinked you and Layla so comprehensively, but there is something sinister and unhinged about the man. It might be time to put his investigators to work."

"Goodness, Maggie, you are your own worst enemy. No man will want to marry a meddling gossip, and that's what you are fast becoming. Be grateful that a man of the Duke's stature is interested in your sister and you. Come along; it is time to leave."

When they entered the ballroom to collect Lydia, the Duke was, as Maggie suspected, standing close to Lydia, preventing others from interacting with her. The Duke gave Maggie a fake smile and said, "Lady Margaret, we missed you. We have time for one more dance, so I'm happy to stand up with you."

Maggie tried to hide her disgust, but how could she decline without offending the man?

"Thank you for your kind offer, but I feel under the weather, and dancing can only make me feel worse."

The Duke raised an eyebrow but didn't call her out on her lie. Turning to her Mother, Maggie asked to leave, and a reluctant Lydia followed.

Chapter Five

Lady Buckingham berated Maggie for the entirety of the carriage trip. Nothing Maggie could say would stop the barrage, so she silently sat with her eyes closed and her mind on more pleasant things. Ben's success with the wallflowers was heartwarming and remarkable, showing that all it takes is one brave person to do the right thing, and others will follow. When the women arrived home, Maggie asked Cummings where her Father was. Her Father was in the library, his favourite room in the house, with a half-empty whisky decanter in front of him. Maggie sighed. Now was not the time to tell her Father of her concerns, but she asked if they could meet after breakfast.

"Is there a problem, Mags?"

"Yes, there is, but I think we both need clear heads to solve the problem, and I, for one, am exhausted. See you in the morning."

After tossing and turning, Maggie fell asleep in the early hours of the morning.

The new day seemed to arrive too soon, but Maggie knew that if she didn't meet with her Father as agreed by late afternoon, he would have retired to his club. Breakfast was a solitary meal; neither her Mother nor Layla had risen, and after confirming with the servers, Maggie knew her Father had eaten and was in his office. When Maggie knocked on the door, her Father told her to come in; she found him with his shirt sleeves rolled up and a stack of paperwork in front of him.

"Ah, Maggie, I guess all did not go well with the ball last night."

As Maggie poured out her woes to her Father, Henry Buckingham listened with a frown.

"So let me get this clear. Lord Windsor, the Duke of Berwick, is interested in one or both of you. Is that right?"

"Yes, and he has warned the other men to steer clear of us, so only my friend Lord Reinholt is game to challenge him. The Duke is a bully and wishes to control both Layla and me. Last night, while I was chatting with a group of friends, he came over and said that Mother needed me urgently, and she had asked him to deliver the message. I looked over to where Mother was standing; she was chatting with Mrs Spencer and did not indicate that she wanted me to return to her side. When I told the man I would make my way over to Mother in a few moments, he grabbed me by the arm and dragged me across the room. Lord Reinholt saved me, and I hid in the retiring room for the rest of the night."

Maggie rolled her sleeve to show her Father the fingerprints the angry Duke had caused.

Henry Buckingham cursed at the sight of his daughter's bruised arm.

"It sounds like I should chat with this blighter and ask his intentions."

"The Duke will need to decide which of us he wants, but let me be clear: if the man asks to court me, the answer is no. I want him to leave me alone and to stop manhandling me. Layla is besotted with the man, but I doubt he would make her happy if they wed, but I can't convince my sister that she should walk away."

"We will discuss this over dinner, but neither you nor Layla will attend whatever function your Mother has agreed to attend tonight. Tell Layla I have vetoed the event tonight, and I will discuss my plan with your Mother. I will write Lord Windsor a note requesting his presence at our house tomorrow, and your Mother can deliver it tonight at the ball."

"Thank you, Father."

Dinner was an awkward meal, and rather than discussing the problem, Maggie had discussed it with her father in front of the servants in the room; Henry dismissed the staff. When he cleared the room, he said, "I guess you wonder what is happening and why I have forbidden you, Layla and Maggie from attending tonight's function. Maggie has brought to my attention some disturbing facts, and we need those cleared up before we can move on."

"What has Maggie said that convinced you to cancel our outing?" Lord Buckingham frowned.

"Layla, is Lord Windsor interested in you or Maggie?"

Layla blushed. "I'm not sure."

Lady Buckingham said, "What does it matter which of the girls he is interested in?"

"It matters because, from what Maggie said, the man has warned off all other prospective suitors, and when he finally makes his decision, the eligible men will have moved on, and one of our daughters will need a second season to find a husband."

"How would Maggie know Lord Windsor threatened the other gentlemen?"

"If you have watched any of the dances, you will realise that Lord Reinholt refuses to ignore me, and he was the person who informed me of the Duke's decree."

Phyllis Buckingham sprang to the defence of Lord Windsor. "You would take the word of a worthless nobody over that of a Duke? Maggie, I told you to dissuade the man, not to form an alliance with him. You can't trust his word regarding the Duke because Reinholt wants you and is scared Lord Windsor will choose to court you."

"Is that true, Maggie?"

"Father, Mother is so focused on marrying us off that she has become fixated on a relationship based on friendship. The first time I danced with Ben, he explained that he was a second son without the need or desire to find a wife. I confided that I would not marry the first eligible man I met, so we decided to enjoy each other's company. He is easy to talk to and amusing, and despite what the snobs in the ton believe, his late Father set him up for the future. It is not my place to divulge his plans, but he is far from destitute. He is well versed with the goings on as a man circulating in the crowds at a ball, so his information is solid."

Layla looked agitated. "If that's true, why would he do that?"

Maggie said, "Because the Duke hasn't decided which of us he wants, he wants to cut down the competition while he leaves us wondering. I detest the man; he is controlling and a bully, and if I could convince you to see the real him, then you wouldn't want him either. Layla, you are the only sister in the running, regardless of who he wants."

Lady Buckingham looked fit to swoon, and Maggie decided to impart uplifting news.

"Father, do you remember I asked about the wallflowers?"

"Yes, I'm not in my dotage yet."

"Well, something good has happened. When the marriage mart mammas realised that Ben was a second son, they herded him away from their daughters, and I was the only debutante who would dance with him. When I pointed out to him that the wallflowers suffered from the same bias he did, he took it upon himself to introduce himself to the ladies and explain that he was not looking for a wife, but wanted to enjoy dancing and socialising. Almost as soon as Ben began dancing and chatting to the wallflowers, a group of men who were rich enough not to care about dowries started to ask the women to dance. Gentlemen are courting two ladies, and the others are enjoying their season for the first time."

"This friend of yours sounds like he is an honourable fellow. Maybe I should meet him?"

"Please, Father, don't ask him his intentions regarding me because if you do, it will ruin our friendship."

Henry nodded. "Understood, dear daughter. Phyllis, you have the letter I wrote for Lord Windsor. If you give it to him, you can leave whenever you want. Go to bed, girls. Tomorrow is a new day, and we will sort out this mess with luck."

Chapter Six

The following morning, Lord Windsor, the Duke of Berwick, arrived for his meeting with Lord Buckingham. Lord Buckingham scrutinised the fellow who had caused discord and confusion among the female members of his family. After exchanging cordial greetings, they took their seats in the library's armchairs.

"As you probably know, I asked you here today to ask about your intentions towards my daughters. Never before have I seen a prospective suitor pay attention to two ladies simultaneously."

The Duke gave a smile and shook his head.

"My Lord, never have I met two more different but equally entrancing young ladies. You are correct that it is unusual to entertain two ladies at once, but I find it hard to decide which of your lovely daughters to choose as my Duchess."

"Your Grace, I can make the choice more straightforward for you; Maggie has informed me that she does not wish to have you court her, so there is no longer a choice."

The Duke's face turned red, and Henry Buckingham wondered whether it resulted from anger or embarrassment.

"Well, it's a relief to know I won't break somebody's heart by choosing between the girls. If Layla is agreeable, I would like to court her."

"Before you go, I wish to discuss other things with you. You may be a Duke, but your behaviour towards my daughters was distasteful. Warning off other prospective suitors while you dally over your choice is unheard of and potentially harmful for the girl not chosen as your prospective Duchess. While you lingered over your choice, other suitors had moved on and made liaisons with available debutantes. Your actions may mean that Maggie has to return next season to make a match, a cost that I can afford but would prefer not to outlay."

"Lord Buckingham, I resent the accusation that my actions were underhanded. Other gentlemen may have given your daughters a wide berth because they knew they couldn't compete with all I have to offer a wife."

The Duke's supercilious smirk verified, in Henry Buckingham's mind, Maggie's opinion of the man.

"I have one last concern. I will call you out, Duke or not, if I find bruises you inflict on Maggie again. Now that you have made your choice, she is not your responsibility. I urge you to leave her alone."

Henry asked Carruthers to call his family to meet him in the sitting room when the tense meeting ended. As he waited for the women, he contemplated the Duke's behaviour. Maggie said that the man was a controlling bully, and he had seen no hint of an apology for the treatment of his daughters. Henry was inclined to believe Lord Reinholt's information regarding the avoidance by other suitors towards his daughters. He was unsure about allowing the man to court Layla, but last night, when they spoke, it seemed that she had taken a liking to him.

When the ladies entered, Lady Buckingham instructed Carruthers to send a maid with refreshments and then settled down to hear what her husband had to say.

"As you probably know, I have met with Lord Windsor and given him the information that Maggie would not welcome his courtship; he has chosen you, Layla, as his prospective Duchess."

Layla squealed with excitement, and her Mother hugged her. Henry Buckingham drew in a deep breath before beginning to speak.

"I know you want this man, Layla, but I'm concerned that he is not what he seems. Maggie's assessment was proven today when he glibly tried to excuse his behaviour of pushing other suitors away and monopolising you two."

Layla pouted. "Why does Maggie have to approve of my suitor? Will I be allowed to approve when Maggie finds someone? She took a dislike to Lord Windsor from the second time we encountered him and has done everything she can to torment him."

Maggie shook her head. "Layla, you can have an opinion on my suitor when I find a suitable man, and I am not stopping you from being with this man. You are correct that I disapproved of him trying to corral us and stop us from dancing with other gentlemen, but after his bullying behaviour towards me, I detest the man. The Duke is a controlling bully, and I don't doubt he will cut you off from family and friends once you are under his control and minimise your social outings. I am worried about you. I am glad Father sees what I see."

Lady Buckingham interrupted. "I, for one, am glad to see Layla has secured a prestigious suitor and look forward to the wedding preparations. Since the man has made his choice, I suggest you, Maggie, do something about finding a suitor for yourself."

Maggie's dislike of Layla's chosen suitor placed a strain on the previously harmonious relationship between the girls. After Layla's parents announced her engagement to the Duke, the girls journeyed to the next social event. They didn't converse, and the trip was uncomfortable for all of them. Once the women moved from the foyer to the ballroom, they stood for a moment, taking in their surroundings. When Maggie felt a strange sensation on her neck, she turned to find Lord Winsor standing uncomfortably close and glaring at her. She shivered at the fury emanating from his eyes; her refusal to be involved in his insulting competition for his favour had not gone down well.

Maggie looked around the room, searching for a familiar face to rescue her. When she saw Lord Reinholt, Maggie smiled and walked towards him.

"Good evening, Lady Maggie. Why the concerned face?"

"Is that cad Windsor still glaring at me? I refused to compete for his favour and left the running for Layla, so he is incensed."

"Why is your sister blinded to the man's true nature?"

"Mothers worldwide insist that the best thing that can happen to their daughters is to marry a man with a title. They feed us that drivel from childhood, so when some ladies reach the social whirl, they believe they need a man with a title, regardless of his personality or character."

"Well, Lady Maggie, the dancing is about to start. Let me select the third dance and the supper waltz, and with luck, other gentlemen will realise you are a free agent and fill in the spaces."

Ben was right; gentlemen who had previously shied away wrote their names on her card, and the night progressed pleasantly. As she chatted with her last partner, she felt the man step back, and the same crawling sensation she had felt earlier returned. The next dance was a waltz, and as Maggie frantically looked around for her partner, a hand landed on her arm.

Maggie attempted to shrug off Lord Windsor's grasp, but he moved closer to her and said, "I believe this is my dance."

"No, I have another partner; something must have delayed him."

"He isn't delayed; he is not coming. I convinced him to find another partner."

"No, my Father told you to leave me alone."

"But your Mother loves me, and she thought we should reconcile our differences during the dance. It doesn't look right if you avoid me all night."

Maggie cursed her mother inwardly as she followed Lord Windsor onto the dance floor. When the band struck up the number, he moved her with fluidity through the packed area until they were alone on the edge of the dance floor.

"Your Grace, please direct us closer to the other dances."

"Not a chance, sweetheart; I have plans for you."

Maggie's pulse picked up, and her fear of him increased. What could he do to her in such a public place? She knew too well what he could do when his hand landed on her derriere, and he rubbed the lush globes.

"Stop, damn you. Stop!"

The Duke chuckled as he yanked her hard against him. She could feel his enlarged manhood through her thin dress, and even though she struggled, Maggie couldn't free herself.

"Don't pretend you are a pure maiden. A woman who wears a dress that reveals so much of her breasts is not an innocent but a temptress. Did you know every man who has danced with you tonight has looked down your dress and enjoyed the view of your breasts?"

As Maggie struggled, praying for the music to end, the Duke chuckled.

"I am enjoying your ministrations, but I think you would enjoy it more if I pushed you up against the back wall and took you where you stood. A quarrelsome piece like you would enjoy it hard and rough."

When the music stopped, Maggie was ready to swoon. With tears running down her face, she bolted for the door and huddled in a corner when she reached the retiring room. Thinking of what Lord Windsor did and what he said turned Maggie's stomach, and she heaved the contents into a nearby chamber pot. God, she felt violated and desperately needed a bath to wash the man's odour from her body. How could she return to the dance floor and pretend everything was alright? Her Father would kill the man if he discovered what he had done, and Maggie would lose her sister and Father if she told them both of his assault. She had no alternative but to return to the dance and pretend everything was good. From here on, Maggie would keep a wide berth from the deranged man, and if he came near her again, despite the scandal she would cause, she would scream before she let him touch her again.

When Maggie returned to the ballroom, it was with relief that she realised her next dance was with Ben. She felt terrible that she had stood up other gentlemen when she had her breakdown in the retiring room, but intended to apologise, citing a dizzy feeling that made her rest for a while.

"Maggie, you are as stiff as a board. Are you well?"

"No, I'm not, but your company always cheers me up."

During supper, Maggie searched for her Mother to beg to go home, but she and her sister seemed to have disappeared.

"Ben, I am not well. I want to go home. Will you escort me to the entry? I can't see Mother or Layla, but I can ask the driver to return for them."

Chapter Seven

"Where did you go last night? Lord Windsor saw you leaving with that neér do well I told you to dissuade."

Her Mother's attack, almost before Maggie sat at the table, pulled her up short. Anger boiled in Maggie's brain, and she shouted at her Mother.

"If you had bothered to check on me at any time during the night, instead of swanning around bragging to other mothers that Layla had bagged the Duke, you might have realised that I was ill. Please correct me if I'm wrong, but I mistakenly thought you were there to escort Layla and me. Instead, you stand guard over your precious charge and her intended. While you were complaining about Ben, he realised I was unwell and organised for me to go home."

Her Father entered the breakfast room with a frown.

"What is the shouting about? I swear the servants in the kitchen can hear you."

Lady Buckingham sniffed. "I merely asked Maggie where she got to with that neér do well last night."

Maggie, riled beyond belief, retaliated.

"No, you did not ask me anything; you accused me of leaving with Ben because the always honourable and truthful Duke said he saw us go together. If you had asked, instead of accusing me, there would be no need for raised voices. I'm frustrated that you and Layla are oblivious to his malevolent nature and intrusive behaviour, and I'm even more upset that he's come between Layla and me. How you fawn over him,

Mother, makes me ill, and how he and Layla come before me every time saddens me. I am going for a walk, and if we have callers, tell them I'm not receiving."

Lord Buckingham watched his daughter leave, concern shadowing his eyes. He watched as his wife ignored her oldest daughter's departure and initiated a conversation with Layla.

"Lady Buckingham, was what Maggie said the truth? If she were ill, I assume she looked for you but couldn't find you. Are you too busy to adequately chaperone both of our daughters? My question would be, where were you when Maggie needed you?"

Layla glanced at her Mother and came to her aid.

"Um, last night Lord Windsor wanted to show me his new carriage and how well sprung it is. He took Mother and me for a short drive."

Henry Buckingham glared at his wife. "So Maggie was right; you are too busy with one daughter to escort the other. As for your endless comments about Lord Benjamin Reinholt, I made enquiries, and as Maggie said, the man is certainly not impoverished."

Intent on leaving the house, Layla asked Cummings to find a footman to accompany her and asked her maid to join them. Maggie was unwilling to walk alone, scared that the Duke might follow her and make good on his threats of last night. Was she to live in fear for years until the man moved away or until she found a husband who could defend her? The quiet streets she traversed calmed Maggie's nerves, but accompanied by her servants, she began questioning her life. While she attended many social functions, she had no friends because most debutantes considered each other adversaries. The girls were all hunting for the perfect husband, and friendships in that situation didn't survive. A few of the most beautiful or sought-after girls formed alliances, but ordinary girls like Maggie had little to offer in the way of connections to pave her way. She wondered what had drawn Lord Windsor to pay attention to Layla and her, but she couldn't rejoice in a toxic relationship with that man.

With dread, Maggie thought of the upcoming ball at Lady Osbourne's home. How could she avoid the Duke? Even if she moved out of his sphere of influence, he made it his task to drag her back to his side. The horror of the liberties Lord Windsor took while they waltzed made Maggie feel nauseated and dirty. On arriving home the night before, she had ordered a bath and scrubbed every inch of her body before falling into bed, only to cry herself to sleep. Maggie had toyed with telling her Father of the Duke's abhorrent behaviour, but feared that if he called the man out, he might die in his attempt to defend her honour. Even if the Duke did not maim her Father, the reason for the duel would filter through to the ton, and despite being the victim, it would ruin her. Reluctantly, Maggie turned for home, knowing that whatever her reason, her Mother would insist she attend the ball.

Maggie silently sat in the carriage as her Mother and sister chatted about the upcoming function. Lord Windsor had reluctantly loosened the reins on Layla at her Father's insistence, and she glowed at the thought of the upcoming dances. Maggie could find nothing to look forward to; the crush, the overpowering scent of perfumes and the ever-present threat of Lord Windsor made her want to hide in the retiring room for the evening. Thinking to cheer, her sister Layla said, "If you are short on dance partners tonight, I'm sure Lord Windsor would dance with you if I asked."

Maggie shuddered and said, "Layla, your offer is kind, but I don't wish to dance with your intended. I have already said that I dislike the man and would rather sit out than be in his company."

Lady Buckingham frowned. "Layla's offer is generous, and you would be a fool to reject her suggestion."

"Mother, I have expressed my distaste at the man, and while Layla's beau doesn't have to meet my approval, it is not incumbent on me to socialise with him. Layla, please do not suggest that the man ask me to dance, as I will decline his offer, even though debutantes are not supposed to refuse a man's invitation. Save us all the embarrassment and forget your suggestion."

More conversation was interrupted as the carriage drew to a halt at the entrance to the mansion. Other carriages lined the driveway, and the Buckingham women sat in their carriage, waiting for their turn to enter the house. When their turn came, the butler introduced the women, and they chatted with their hosts before moving into the ballroom.

Maggie looked around, hoping to see her friend Ben, but her eyes widened as she saw Lord Windsor striding towards their family group. Without considering social protocols, Maggie slipped behind her Mother and sister and made for the other side of the room. As she mingled in the crowd, she kept a lookout for the Duke, but at the moment, she appeared to have evaded him. Acquaintances approached and, after some polite chit-chat, pencilled their names onto her dance card. Even as she chatted, she watched for Ben's arrival, and her face lit up when she saw him approaching. He winked as he took her hand and bowed politely.

"Lady Maggie, you look lovely tonight. I hope you have unfilled spaces on your dance card."

With relief, Maggie handed over her card, and Ben pencilled his name into the space for the supper waltz.

"Even if these gentlemen dance with you all night, I will have your undivided attention during supper. If you'll excuse me, I must go over and pencil in some dances with the lovely ladies along the wall."

Maggie watched Ben weave his way through the crowd, and she gave thanks to the stars that aligned the night she met her friend. The snobby debutantes had no idea what they were missing, and truthfully, Maggie was glad that she didn't have to share him with them.

Dance after dance distracted Maggie, and while she enjoyed herself, no one caught her eye. Where was the man whom she might consider as a husband? Watching Layla fall for the Duke, Maggie swore riches or a title wouldn't sway her. Layla was so smitten by the Duke that telling her about his assault would push them further apart because her sister would think her accusations were a means to sever her arrangement with the Duke. Knowing what she did about the Duke caused her concern for her sister's future, but Maggie had clarified her feelings, and she could do nothing more.

Chapter Eight

After two more social occasions where Maggie avoided the Duke, she relaxed, assuming he had moved his unwanted attention to her sister. They were to attend Lady Herring's ball, a celebration of her daughter's betrothal to an Earl from the southern section of the country. Lady Buckingham accepted the invitations from society's most well-known hostesses, and much to Maggie's disgust, these events were always a crush. Why jamming people into a room where there was barely room to move and the air was always oppressive baffled Maggie, and she vowed that if she ever became a hostess of note, she would restrict the number of her guests to a comfortable level.

Maggie's evasive tactics to avoid Lord Windsor seemed to be working, and the gentlemen he threatened while he decided which of the Buckingham girls to court had returned. A break in her commitments allowed Maggie to move to the balcony. The fresh air revived her, and with supper only fifteen minutes away, she decided to remain on the terrace until the supper crush eased. The view over the garden was delightful, with lanterns lining the pathways and potted shrubs scattered over the lawns. A prickling feeling crawled across her neck, and she turned to discover Lord Windsor standing behind her.

"What do you want?"

"Ah, Maggie, why so hostile?"

"I have never given you the right to call me by my first name. Please leave; I came here to get some fresh air and resent your intrusion."

Lord Windsor chuckled. "Well, blame the intrusion on your sister. She asked me to dance the supper waltz with you, and then we can eat supper together."

"If what you say is true, my sister oversteps the mark. Regardless of the truth of your explanation, I will not dance with you tonight or ever again. If you imagine I would ever place myself in your clutches again, you must think me a fool."

Lord Windsor's smirk vanished as he approached Maggie.

"Don't play hard to get, Maggie dear. Come along like a good girl."

Maggie backed away with little hope that she could avoid the grasping hands of the Duke.

"Get away, or I will scream. I would rather people consider me ruined than be subjected to your inappropriate groping and lewd comments."

As Lord Windsor grabbed her arm and began to pull her towards the dance floor, Maggie struggled.

The deep voice of a man shattered the moment.

"Let the lady go."

Lord Windsor's face reddened either in anger or embarrassment, and Maggie didn't care which, if the gentleman behind her could force the Duke to let her go.

"Mind your own business."

The Duke pulled on Maggie's arm, and the man behind moved close, and a click revealed a blade embedded in his cane.

"This altercation is my business because I have sat here listening to this lady refusing your advances, which appear unwanted. Let her arm go, or I will slice your pretty face, and the other ladies won't think you such a good catch."

"Do you know who I am?"

"It appears that you are an aristocrat who believes his status allows him to molest young ladies. Leave the lady alone and go back to her misguided sister."

The Duke used his leverage on Maggie's arm to shove her away from him as he stalked back into the ballroom. As Maggie staggered from the shove, her saviour steadied her and guided her to a seat. Shaking violently after her altercation with the Duke, Maggie gave the man next to her a wan smile.

"Thank you."

"You're welcome. I assume from your comments that the man has forced you to dance at another venue and not acted as a gentleman should?"

As Maggie's nerves settled, she directed her attention to the man beside her. He wore a red dress coat of an army officer and tight, cream-coloured pants. His black hair hung over his coat collar, and his amber eyes gleamed on the darkened terrace. Maggie laughed nervously and said, "Well, we have disregarded protocol in speaking to one another before someone has introduced us, but in the circumstances, I am willing to flaunt the rules. I am Lady Margaret Buckingham. My friends call me Maggie, and I count you as a friend in this situation."

The wickedly handsome military man said, "Captain Theo Devine at your service, ma'am."

When he took her hand, Maggie felt tingling, something she had never experienced with any of the men who had greeted her. Maggie blushed and watched his lips curl up at the sides. Was he laughing at her? Her only consolation was that the smile never became a full-blown grin, and she ignored it.

"Captain Devine, I have no partner for the supper waltz. Would you be able to accompany me?"

"I am sorry, my lady, but I can't dance."

Maggie looked incredulous.

"How have you made Captain in the army if you aren't able to charm the other officers' wives on the dance floor? Surely someone in the army could teach you to dance."

Captain Devine scrutinised Maggie for a silent minute.

"I have enjoyed talking with you, Lady Maggie, but once I tell you why I can't dance, you will race back to the ballroom like a scalded cat."

"Why don't you try me?"

"I can't dance because my peg leg prevents me from moving freely."

Maggie silently processed what Captain Devine said.

"Your peg leg?"

"Yes."

Maggie's eyes filled with tears.

"So while we all swanned around enjoying ostentatious shows of wealth, you were with the army defending us from an invasion?"

"It would appear so."

Maggie swiped at the tears on her cheeks. "On behalf of all the men who drank smuggled rum and smoked contraband cigars and the women who never gave a thought to the soldiers, I have to say thank you. Your injury does not make you unworthy of consideration, even if you can't dance. And by the way, you'll notice that I haven't raced back to the ballroom."

The Captain grinned. "A truly remarkable feat."

"Considering you can't dance, why come to a ball and sit in the dark on the balcony?"

"Slide over so we are closer to the light. I don't want to ruin your reputation when all we do is talk."

Maggie slid over as requested, but she regretted the loss of contact with the Captain's arm.

"The reason a disabled man would come to a ball is that I am acting as my sister's chaperone. My sister was due to enter society when my Mother became ill. With no close aunts or cousins who could step in, we had to cancel the season or use me as a chaperone. My sister tries to stay within sight, and I sit on the terrace or balcony where I can see her but remain unobtrusive."

"Not only are you an honourable man for defending our country, but you are a kind brother. The waltz has finished; will you have supper with me? And you can tell me about your cane."

Captain Devine rose and held out his elbow for Maggie.

"It would be my pleasure to escort you to supper."

When Captain Devine loaded up their plates, Maggie laughed. As they settled at a table, the Captain said, "What are you laughing at?"

Maggie shook her head. "The first night we came to a ball, my Mother suggested that Layla and I eat a little before we went because gentlemen didn't like ladies who ate like navies, so that supper would be a light meal. I felt sick with nerves, so I didn't eat, and at supper, my Mother dished a few morsels and said that was enough. I'm sure every man who danced with me after supper was appalled by my rumbly stomach."

Captain Devine grinned. "I believe supper is our reward for attending these overcrowded events. Unless your Mother is behind us, I suggest you eat up."

Maggie looked over her shoulder, but her Mother and Layla were nowhere in sight.

Chapter Nine

Much to Maggie's disappointment, Captain Devine retired to his watching post when supper finished, and Maggie danced with the men who had signed her card. While she smiled politely at her partners, the dashing Captain remained on her mind. What was it about Captain Devine that made butterflies take flight in her stomach? She admitted that the man was handsome, but it went deeper than good looks. Heaven knows there were enough fine specimens in their best clothes parading around the dance floor, but none appealed. She had eaten supper with other partners, but, except for Ben, she never got caught up in the conversation and never wanted to spend more time with any of them.

As the night ended, Maggie scanned the guests for her Mother or Layla but could not locate them in the diminishing crowd. Wrapping her shawl around her shoulders, Maggie exited the building and approached the footman marshalling the departing carriages. The footman's casual response to the location of her family carriage shocked her.

"What do you mean, my family left after supper? Surely they sent the carriage back for me?"

"I'm sorry, Lady Margaret, but I don't question the toffs, especially the likes of Lord Windsor."

"How am I supposed to return home?"

"When the guests' carriages clear the driveway, I could try to hire a handsome cab for you."

The deep voice of her rescuer interrupted her dialogue with the footman.

"Is there a problem?"

"My family have left and didn't send the carriage back for me. The footman will try to hire a handsome cab, but I must wait until the guests have all left. I doubt I have enough to pay a driver."

Maggie wrung her hands, her distress evident even to the casual observer.

"Let me take you home. My sister would love to meet another debutante who doesn't consider her the enemy, and with her present, we will observe good etiquette."

When Maggie nodded, Captain Devine flipped some coins to the footman and thanked him for attempting to solve Maggie's problem. The ladies' introduction went smoothly, and before they arrived at Buckingham's townhouse, the girls had organised to meet on the morrow for a stroll in the park. Maggie's good mood lasted until Cummings opened the door for her.

"Miss Maggie, your parents are in the sitting room and ask that you call there before retiring."

Maggie laid her reticule on the hallway table and followed Cummings to the sitting room. The butler opened the door for her, and Maggie was surprised to see her parents and Layla all looking agitated.

"Where the dickens have you been? Your Mother and Layla returned hours ago."

"Goodness me, Maggie, I wouldn't be surprised if you have ruined your good name. When the Dowagers learn you accepted a carriage ride home with a stranger, they will drum you out of society."

Maggie listened in amazement as her parents hurled accusations at her. Before she could defend herself, Layla wailed.

"I know you dislike Lord Windsor, but your behaviour may make him reconsider his courtship."

Maggie crossed her arms and glared at her family.

"Do I get to speak before you resort to stoning me in public?"

Lady Buckingham waved a hand. "Feel free, but I doubt you can rectify the damage you have managed to wreak."

"Tonight, I drove to Lady Herring's ball with you, Mother and Layla. I assumed I would travel home the same way. Just before the supper waltz, Lord Windsor arrived to tell me that you, Layla, said he should dance with me, and we could have supper together. Why would you do that? I told you I despise the man, and you ignored my request not to ask him to dance with me."

"Wait, I never asked him to dance with you because I knew how you felt and didn't want to start a scandal. You must be mistaken."

"Layla, your ability to overlook the bullying and controlling behaviour of the Duke is staggering. Sorry to doubt you, but that was the excuse he used to attempt to force me to dance with him. I declined numerous times, and when he grabbed my arm to pull me onto the dance floor, a man sitting in the shadows intervened and sent the cad on his way. I looked for you, Mother and Layla during supper, but couldn't see you. Imagine my distress when I tried to leave, and the footman told me you had left but hadn't sent the carriage back for me."

"Why would we? Lord Windsor said you told him you had organised a ride home with a suitor."

"Did you forget I despise the man? Why would I tell him anything? Lord Windsor lied to you. He wanted to pay me back for refusing to dance with him, and what better way than to leave me stranded?"

"How did you get home?"

"Captain Devine came to my rescue again. He escorted his sister to the ball, and when he realised I was stranded, he offered to bring me home, all nicely chaperoned by his sister. At no time was I alone with a man, and I did not organise to ride with a suitor or anyone else. Do you not know me well enough to question the Duke's statement? Do you believe I would place myself in a compromised position after twenty-one years of training? That you would believe a stranger without question says all I need to know regarding my standing in this family."

Before Maggie could leave the room, Henry Buckingham stopped her.

"This mess sounds like the Duke orchestrated it, and I'm beginning to wonder what game he is playing. But placing that aside, tell me about Captain Devine. Who is the man?"

"His name is Theo Devine; I assume that is short for Theodore. He has a nineteen-year-old sister who is an absolute hoot. I know his Mother is recovering from an illness, so Captain Devine escorted his sister. He fought on the peninsula with Lord Nelson before he sustained an injury, and the doctors sent him home. After the incident with Lord Windsor, I had supper with Captain Devine, and he is intelligent and respectful."

"Maggie, it's all very well; this soldier coming to your aid, but don't become too familiar with the man."

"I hate to tell you, Mother, that I have organised to meet Esme Devine for a stroll in the park tomorrow. It will be nice to have a friend outside the marriage mart. I can take a maid as a chaperone, so everything is proper."

When her Father stood, Maggie bid everyone good night and shuffled to her bedroom. The night's excitement, the incident with the Duke and the abandonment had taken their toll. Hopefully, tomorrow will be a better day. As her maid helped Maggie undress, her mind drifted to the handsome Captain. Regardless of what her Mother said, Maggie hoped to run into the man frequently, especially now that she knew where to look for him at the endless ball she attended.

As she tried to turn off her mind to fall asleep, she remembered the Duke's insistence that she dance with him. She knew what he intended to do during the dance and would never put herself in that position again. She thought back on her Father's words and asked the same question: what game was the Duke playing? There must be a way of avoiding the man, but for the moment, Maggie felt too tired to construct a plan.

45

Chapter Ten

The following day, Maggie carefully selected her outfit and asked her maid to arrange her hair. When she arrived for breakfast, her Mother raised her eyebrows.

"Who are you attempting to impress, your new friend or her brother?"

"Should I race upstairs and find a house dress? I don't even know if Captain Devine will accompany us on our walk."

When breakfast finished, Maggie had to admit to being nervous. Would Captain Devine escort the ladies, or would he send a chaperone? Did his wooden leg prevent him from walking for pleasure? While sitting in the parlour, waiting for a carriage to arrive, Maggie heard a knock on the front door. A male voice made her quirk her brows; that didn't sound like Captain Devine, so he must have sent a driver. Cummings opened the parlour door to let the visitor enter when Maggie realised the voice belonged to the despised Duke; Maggie leapt from her seat.

"I will tell Layla you are here."

"No reason to hurry; you and I can chat while we wait."

" Being alone in a room with you is not something I would choose to do."

Maggie bolted through the door and located Cummings as he stepped from the next room.

"Have you lost your mind? In whose world would you imagine me being alone in a room with a predator like the Duke was a good idea? I should let my Father know you have no regard for his daughter's reputation."

Cummings blustered. "I didn't think it was a good idea, but the Duke ordered me to close the door. What was I to do?"

"Grab a maid or the housekeeper and shove her into the room next time. Do not ever leave me alone with that man."

Before Cummings could answer, a couple of things happened at once. Layla walked into the hallway to meet the Duke, who had left the parlour, and someone knocked on the door. After greeting his intended, the Duke looked at Maggie and said, "Are you ready to go?"

Maggie frowned. "Ready to go?"

"Yes, you are our chaperone today. Your Mother is under the weather and said we could take you with us."

Maggie laughed as she turned to the door. "I told Mother I was having a stroll in the park, and I am certainly not chaperoning you two. Get a maid, get a footman; I don't give a toss who chaperones you, but it won't be me. My ride is here, so enjoy yourselves."

Maggie could hear the Duke cursing as she slid her hand through the Captain's outstretched arm and walked towards his carriage.

Once Captain Devine helped Maggie to enter the coach, she greeted her new friend. The ride to the park gave Esme and Maggie time to get reacquainted, and as there was no maid to escort them, Maggie deduced that Captain Devine intended to accompany the ladies. The weather was sunny, and Maggie was glad she had worn a bonnet, although Esme used a parasol. Captain Devine let the girls chatter together, walking stoically beside them. Maggie glanced at him occasionally, concerned that the walking was too difficult for him, but he showed no signs of discomfort. A vacant park bench provided an excuse to rest, and Maggie wondered if now was the time to ask for help from her new friends.

"I was hoping you two might be able to offer some suggestions. Captain, did you tell Esme how we met?"

"No, I didn't. I wasn't sure what happened between you and the Duke before our altercation, but you don't seem like a hysterical person, so I guess there must be a backstory. Esme was curious, but I didn't think it was my story to tell."

"At the start of the season, Layla and I had many dance partners, but when the Duke arrived, the partners disappeared. The only person we had to dance with was the Duke. My friend, Lord Reinholt, ignored the man and continued to have two dances with me at each event, and he told me that the Duke had warned other suitors to keep their distance."

As the story unfolded, Maggie watched her friends' faces. She saw the Captain's fists clenched when she retold them the story of the first and only waltz she had shared with the Duke. Esme's look of horror gave Maggie a moment of regret for subjecting this innocent to her tale, but she needed to tell someone, and who better than the man who saved her? When she finished her account, she said. "How am I to avoid the cad? He attends the same social outings that Mother, Layla and I attend, and I'm becoming a nervous wreck watching for him and trying to avoid him."

Esme answered first. "Have you told your Father about the man's behaviour?"

"I considered it, but if he calls the Duke out, Father could die or sustain a severe injury, and even if Father won, the reason for the duel would spread through the ton like wildfire; it would surely ruin me."

Captain Devine had remained quiet during the recount, but now he made a suggestion.

"If you confided in your Father that you are uncomfortable with the Duke, would he allow you to attend different events? I know everyone chooses the premier balls and soirees, but lesser ladies are hosting those who choose not to be part of the crush at a ball. I only survive those affairs because I sit out of the way, but if I were in the midst of things, I would choose other venues."

"I could ask Father, but then I would have to go alone. I wonder whether Lord Reinhart might accompany me because he isn't actively seeking a partner?"

Esme raised her eyebrows. "Change the subject briefly, and tell me about your relationship with Lord Reinhart."

Maggie smiled. "At the first occasion we attended, Ben asked to dance, and his opening statement was that while he enjoyed dancing and socialising, he wasn't looking for a wife. I explained that I wasn't desperate enough to accept the first offer from a man, and we decided to remain friends. He is tricky to dance with because he makes me laugh, and as you know, Esme, laughing is against the rules."

"Did I notice him dancing with the wallflowers? What is that about?"

"Because Ben is a second son and the marriage mart Mothers want wealth and a title for their daughters, they have refused to allow him to dance with their precious daughters. The joke is on them because Ben is extremely wealthy, but he keeps that under wraps because he wants a wife who desires him, not a wealthy lifestyle."

When Maggie explained why Ben danced with the wallflowers, Esme shook her head.

"So, not just a handsome man, but a decent one as well.What a novelty."

Captain Devine rose from his seat.

"It must be time to return, but I'm unsure if we have been of much assistance."

"Theo, could we accompany Maggie to some of the lesser affairs? I have not found one gentleman that interests me, and I don't care about a title or wealth so that those other occasions might be a reprieve from the crushes and snobbery."

"Do you think your mother will approve?"

"She wants me to be happy. She has no high hopes of a title or immense wealth, so I believe she will approve."

As the Captain escorted the women back to their carriage, he seated them, and as the driver moved off, he said, "Could we meet again tomorrow to look at the other options for our evenings out? Would your parents approve of you joining Esme and Mother for morning tea? She is improving, and I'm sure she would enjoy some company."

"Thank you, I will ask."

When the Captain helped Maggie alight from the carriage, he squeezed her hand.

"Chin up, my lady; it will all work out."

Chapter Eleven

As Maggie entered the house, Cummings waited until Maggie had removed her hat before he hesitantly spoke.

"My lady, we have a problem that I believe you may be able to solve."

"I will try, but why don't you take your problem to my Mother? She deals with the servants."

"With respect, Miss Maggie, I don't believe your Mother will fix the problem. Can you accompany me to the kitchen?"

Maggie followed the butler, curious but unconcerned. What could be so wrong that the man brought the problem to her? When they entered the kitchen, Maggie raised startled eyebrows; every member of the household staff stood in the room.

"Goodness, this problem must be of genuinely epic proportions if it concerns everyone. Who is the spokesperson? Please, let's deal with whatever concerns you all have."

Mrs Beasley, the housekeeper, cleared her throat.

"Miss Maggie, the maids are concerned about Lord Windsor's presence in the house."

Maggie nodded. "In confidence, I hate the man too, but with Layla almost engaged to the blighter, his presence will become more frequent."

The kitchen maid, Beau, spoke. "Miss, you don't understand. Lord Windsor thinks the maids are provided for his entertainment, if you get my meaning. His Mother, the Dowager Duchess, can't hire girls as

51

maids at her home after he forced himself on two of the staff. The first girl, Meg, had a boyfriend who stepped up and married her, but the other maid, Elsie, struggles to raise a baby alone. Her parents sent her to the house so her wages could help feed her siblings, but now they are all as poor as church mice and often have nothing to eat. It's criminal, but the magistrate refused to believe the girls, and the Duke said they wanted his attention."

"And if the magistrate wouldn't believe them, why would my mother?"

Maggie took a deep breath as she considered her options.

"First thing. We need to move the girl and her baby here. Cookie, could you use extra help in the kitchen?"

"Yes, ma'am, I could."

"It will be tricky with a baby, but we might be able to find some help in the village. Where is this girl, and how soon could I send a coach for her?"

As the servants and Maggie worked out the details, Maggie realised that just removing the single girls would not alleviate the problem of the other siblings.

"If the family are tenant farmers, why are they having trouble feeding their family?"

"Miss, they were tenant farmers, but when they complained to the magistrate about what the Duke did, he evicted them. They are living in the village but have no employment. Mr Briggs, the Father, spends most of his days trying to catch fish or trap rabbits to feed his family."

"So, let's move the girl first, and I will speak to the tenants to see if they have room for another family. As for you girls, there is a new rule. When Lord Windsor arrives, the maids will congregate in the kitchen. If he asks for refreshments, a footman will accompany the maid. The footman will never leave the maid alone, and if the Duke orders him to go, he can say he is there under my instructions to remain with the maid. If somehow the man corners one of you, scream and run."

Once they settled the rescue details, Maggie asked Cummings to send a message to the stables to have a horse saddled for her and to have a groom accompany her. Speed was of the essence, and she would do whatever she could to offer the whole family a better life. Maggie considered telling her Father of her plans, but decided to finalise them before bringing them to her Father's attention. It's not as if he wouldn't notice another family living in the tenanted estate, but he would assume that a relative needed work and the tenants were satisfied with the arrangement.

The following day, Maggie dispatched two farmhands and the working horses and wagon to collect the family. Satisfied she had avoided a catastrophe, Maggie headed to Captain Devine's home. As her carriage stopped, Maggie realised Lord Reinholt had parked his carriage in the driveway. Maggie smiled for the first time since Cummings asked her to join him in the kitchen.

The butler answered the door and escorted Maggie to the breakfast room. She saw her friends leaning over the table, their hands holding invitations. Maggie heaved a sigh of relief; she had collected Mother's discarded invitations but hadn't thought to suggest that yesterday. Everyone greeted her, the gentlemen bowing over her hand, and Esme hugging her.

"Ben, I never expected to see you here. Whose good idea was this?"

Esme blushed. "You spoke so highly of Lord Reinholt that I asked Theo to contact him."

Ben smiled at the compliment. "If this venture is a success, I might suggest some of the wallflowers look into other options apart from the premier places. It makes sense when you think about it."

The four friends sorted through the invitations and decided on four for the week: two balls, a soiree and a picnic. With their decisions made, they retired to the sitting room for morning tea with Lady Devine. Maggie was a little confused. If the Captain's Mother held the title of Lady, why wasn't he a Lord? Lady Devine looked frail, and Maggie could see she was recovering from a severe illness. Esme explained what they were doing with the invitations, and she agreed that sometimes the crush at many of the balls was more trouble than it was worth. Nobody mentioned that the venue changes were to keep Maggie away from her future brother-in-law.

"I heard that your sister has made a good match, Lady Maggie, a Duke no less."

"Please call me Maggie; yes, she and my Mother are happy with the match."

"Do I detect a lack of enthusiasm regarding the match?"

Maggie laughed. "I know where Esme gets her bluntness from. I try to look excited for her, but can't get past his bullying, controlling nature. I believe she will live to regret her haste in allowing him to court her."

"Oh, dear. And your parents are happy about the match?"

"My Father has reservations, but my Mother and Laya are impressed by his title and apparent wealth."

Captain Devine interrupted his Mother.

"Enough questions, Mother or Lady Maggie will believe we invited her so we could obtain all the gossip."

Maggie rose."I have had a lovely time and look forward to meeting you all at Lady Summer's ball, but I need to attend to a problem at home, so I'll take my leave."

Ben rose at the same time. "I'll walk you out, Maggie; I should be going."

He bowed over Lady Devine's and Esme's hands, then held his arm out for Maggie. Theo returned to the sitting room when the butler opened the door for the pair.

"Those two seem very friendly. Are Maggie and Lord Reinbolt courting?"

Esme looked at her brother and said, "No, or so Maggie says."

Theo nodded. "She told me they met at their first affair, and because he wasn't looking for a wife and she wouldn't take the first offer she got, they decided to be friends. Maggie has had some difficulties with her sister's intended, and I think Ben has supported her."

"Yes, she didn't look thrilled when she spoke about him."

Theo nodded. "A title doesn't make a gentleman."

"Talking about gentlemen, why does Maggie call you Captain and not Lord?"

"When I met Maggie, she was in a pickle, and I helped her. I was wearing my dress uniform, and when she called me Captain, I didn't correct her. The debutantes are after money and a title; present company excepted. I don't want a wife who wants my title and cash but can't bear to accompany me because of my leg. I guess I was protecting myself, but I don't believe Maggie is one of those shallow debutantes."

"Does that mean you are serious about Maggie?"

"I don't know; I'm not sure she even sees me as a prospect. She could do better than I; I'll see how it goes."

" Don't underestimate yourself, son. You have a lot to offer a woman."

Chapter Twelve

Maggie was excited about meeting her friends at Lady Beckett's ball and spent extra time on her appearance. Her maid, Clara, was eager to accompany Maggie as her chaperone. Maggie knew that her Mother and Layla were attending a ball at a wealthy, influential hostess's estate, and she hoped they would leave before Ben arrived to collect her. When the knock came at the door, she strained to hear who Cummings was speaking to. A tap on her door suggested that the caller was Lord Reinholt, and her maid's appearance confirmed her thought.

As she descended the stairs to greet Ben in the foyer, another caller knocked on the door. Maggie had just reached Ben when Lord Windsor entered the hallway. At his appearance, her smile faded, and she shuffled closer to Ben.

Lord Windsor smirked as he regarded her, but directed his comment to Ben.

"Lord Reinholt, I was unaware that you were accompanying us. It would have been best to meet us at the ball because Maggie will travel with us in my carriage."

Having been privy to the maids' concern and hearing what Lord Windsor did to the maids at his Mother's house, caused Maggie to screw up her nose at the man.

"My Father has permitted me to attend different social events from my sister, so I will not travel with you. Clara will accompany me as my chaperone. Lord Reinholt, I believe it is time for us to leave."

"Whose event are you attending?"

Maggie smirked. "That's for us to know and you to wonder about. Enjoy your evening, your Grace, because I intend to enjoy myself."

As they departed the entry, Maggie and Ben chuckled as they heard Lord Windsor shouting his anger at Cummings. The stalwart butler would remain calm, and the Duke's temper would flow off him like liquid. Ben helped her climb into the coach, and once they settled, he said, "I'm confident the man is deranged. Who spends so much time obsessing about a woman who will eventually become his sister-in-law?"

"This morning, my staff came to me to discuss a problem. The servants chose me because they knew my Mother would disregard their concerns. The maids are afraid of being in the house with Lord Windsor because he raped two maids in his Mother's employ."

Maggie recounted the story the servants told her and explained the steps she took to help the victims and their families.

"I have made a rule that when the Duke is in the house, the maids should congregate in the kitchen, and if they have to deliver refreshments, a footman has to accompany the maid. Why can't my sister see what type of man she wants to marry? All the riches in the world would never convince me to settle for someone like him."

"I am appalled at his behaviour, but tonight, you are free of him, so let's enjoy ourselves."

And enjoy themselves they did. Maggie and Esme had many partners, and nobody looked down their noses at Ben. During the evening, a group of gentlemen stopped to chat with Lord Devine; the evening was a great success. As she travelled home with Ben and her maid, Maggie felt triumphant for the first time since the spectre of the Duke hung over her.

"Attending less popular events was a great success, Ben. There are no wallflowers at this ball; what a revelation. It shows everyone doesn't need to attend the splashy, opulent balls to have a good evening."

Maggie's optimism and regard for the guests who attended the lesser events dimmed at her second ball. Debutantes flooded towards Theo, and despite chatting with people, not one man asked her to dance. This turnaround in events was confusing, and try as she might, Maggie couldn't explain what had caused the change in the guest's behaviour. Adding further to her concern, Ben suggested inviting his great-aunt as a chaperone for the girls. Would another chaperone prompt Captain Devlin to reconsider his decision to attend? Seated beside Theo during a break, Maggie raised the subject.

"Captain, if Ben asks his aunt to chaperone Esme and me, will you stop attending the affairs with Esme?"

Theo momentarily looked down at his hands and said, "I haven't decided."

"If you choose not to attend, I will miss our talks."

"Maggie, I am fond of you, but I don't think we are a good match. I'm certain any affection you feel for me is gratitude for my assistance. You deserve a better man than me."

Maggie looked at the man she had become enamoured of and then rose from her chair.

"I'm sorry if I embarrassed you, Captain. I'm sure one of the ladies fawning over you will be the one for you."

Maggie walked towards the chairs at the far wall with no dances on her card. Never before had she considered being a wallflower, but it took moving to a small event for that to become her reality. Maggie watched the women take turns to speak to Captain Devine. They laughed, tapped his arm, and sat extra close to the man she wanted. Maggie forced her attention away from the Captain and watched as Esme and Ben danced. Despite Ben's assertion that he was not looking to marry, it seemed that Esme had stolen his heart.

That evening, Maggie ate supper alone; she couldn't bear the good humour of Esme and Ben, and Captain Devine was eating with another woman. Despite their humour and enjoyment of each other's company, her friends knew something had happened between Captain Devine and Maggie.

As they travelled home in the carriage, Maggie told Ben of her reluctance to attend the soiree they had designated as their next social engagement.

"What happened between you and the Captain?"

"I thought we had a connection, but it seems that all I feel for the Captain is gratitude, according to him. While you three enjoyed your evening, mine was an unmitigated disaster. I never imagined that with my dowry, I would be a wallflower. What happened between last week and tonight? Last week, I had dances, and Captain Devine chatted with people, but this week, I had no partner, and the debutantes are busy flirting, blushing and giggling with him."

"Maggie, please come to the soiree. At least give it another chance."

"All right."

The hostess looked down her nose as the four friends arrived. While the woman smiled at the others, her disdain for Maggie was evident. What social rule had she broken? Why were men avoiding her and women whispering behind their fans as she walked past? Despite his insistence that he had no feelings for her, Theo offered his arm as they entered the building. Within moments, a woman had appeared at the Captain's side, and as she slid her arm around his, Theo discarded Maggie and walked away. Esme and Ben walked along the aisle, unaware of what had happened to Maggie. Left alone, she decided that her evening couldn't get worse, and she retreated to spend the evening in the retiring room. Women entering the room gave her a wide berth, but two matrons disparaged her, calling her horrid names and calling her reputation into question. When Esme came looking for her, the evening was over, and there was nothing to do but return home. Tonight, the friends shared a coach, and they dropped Maggie off first. As they drove away from her home, Esme rounded on her brother.

"What is wrong with you? Not only are you behaving shamelessly with the kind of debutantes you always said you hated, but you've broken Maggie's heart."

"She deserves better than me, Esme. I thought she would find someone else if she believed I was interested in another woman."

Ben snorted. "Good thinking, Captain. For some reason, the ton treats her like a hussy, and ignoring her only makes it worse. You walked in with her this evening; how did she spend the entire evening in the retiring room?"

The Captain ignored the question as he looked out the window. Sighing, he said, "The Babcock deb greeted me and grabbed my arm. I left Maggie to walk in by herself."

The silence of the other two occupants of the coach expressed their horror at his treatment of their friend.

"Do we still attend the picnic or call it quits?"

During the week, Maggie contacted Ben to inform him that she wouldn't attend the picnic. Her walks in the park were a thing of the past, and when people called at the house, Maggie hid in her room. It was too hard to venture out in public without knowing why people hurled insults at her. Had Captain Devine heard rumours about her and pulled back rather than be caught up in a scandal? Maggie dared not even visit Esme for fear of seeing Theo and having to suffer his avoidance of her.

Chapter Thirteen

The hostess warmly welcomed Esme Ben and Theo upon their arrival at the picnic venue. They discovered that the event wasn't a traditional picnic where everyone sat on rugs, but a more sophisticated affair, with the staff spreading small tables across the manor house's grassy gardens. The change in tradition pleased Theo because the thought of being seated on a rug for the duration of the ceremony concerned him.

The trio had only sat at their chosen table when two girls arrived, seeking Theo's attention. As the girls preened and giggled, Esme rolled her eyes. When Ben greeted the girls —a tactic to distract them, Esme felt sure —the women took their eyes off Theo and looked at Esme and Ben.

"Ah, we see you've left the hussy behind. I can't imagine why you brought her with you last time; what kind of reception did she expect?"

Theo glared at the girls. "I beg your pardon?"

"The cat is out of the bag, Captain. A little birdie told us that even though you are a captain, you're extremely wealthy, and your other companion is no better than she should be. We heard that while Lord Windsor tried to decide between the two sisters, the hussy seduced him. He decided she wouldn't be a faithful wife, so he chose the sister."

Ben and Theo rose, "If I find the person spreading such vile rumours, I would call them out. Sorry, ladies, I'm as poor as a church mouse. The stories about Lady Maggie are disgusting and untrue, and I'd thank you for passing that information on to the rest of the guests."

Esme stood. "Let's leave. I don't want to mix with people who choose to ruin a woman's reputation."

As they headed for the exit, a buzz of conversation followed them. When the hostess saw they were leaving, she hurried over to discover the problem.

"Is there a problem?"

Ben turned to face the woman. "There most certainly is. We couldn't figure out why Captain Devine suddenly became so popular until one of the debs told us that someone had told them he was rich. Worse still, your guests are circulating a blatant lie about Lady Maggie. Ruining a debutante's reputation without any proof is criminal. We will not stay here to listen to people whispering lies and rumours like they are the truth."

In the carriage, they covered the first part of the journey in stunned silence. Esme was the first to speak.

"Now we know why the guests shunned Maggie at the last two affairs, but who would put out awful rumours like that?"

Ben and Theo looked at each other, and Theo spoke.

"Without a doubt, the misinformation about me and the lies about Maggie came from the Duke. It's payback for attending events she knew he wouldn't attend. Where do we go with this information?"

"Maggie didn't tell me exactly what happened the first time she waltzed with the Duke, but her distress and avoidance of the man speak for themselves."

"Before we ask to talk to her Father, I need to tell you, Ben, something that I'll have to share with Maggie. When I met Maggie, she called me Captain, and I've never corrected her, but I am Lord Theodore Devine, Earl of Edensburgh."

Ben laughed. "I appreciate the honesty, but I already knew. If your Mother is Lady Devine, it means that you are Lord Devine since your Father passed away. I have one question: how are you going to talk to

Maggie? I imagine she doesn't want anything to do with you after last week's happenings."

"Esme will invite her for morning tea, and I will intercept Maggie on her way to the sitting room. She may not forgive me for causing her pain, but I want to tell her what has happened, and then we will return to the sitting room where we can sort out this mess caused by that blackguard Windsor."

When the invitation from Esme arrived, Maggie considered declining, but as Esme was one of the few people who hadn't shunned her, Maggie decided to make an effort and go. The thought of seeing Captain Devine worried her, but considering his sudden popularity with the ladies of the ton, he was probably visiting and wouldn't be home. Maggie's nerves jiggled as she reached for the brass knocker on the door. Upon hearing her name, the butler asked Maggie to wait, and as he left the entry, Captain Devine entered. As he approached, she dropped her head; was she to be subjected to another barrage of insults?

"Lady Maggie, may I have a few moments of your time?"

"I can't imagine what you had to say; you summed up your feelings well the other night."

"Please, Maggie, let me explain. Will you walk with me in the garden? When I finish, if you wish, I will leave. Give me a moment to find a maid to accompany us."

The garden they entered was protected from the wind by a high brick wall, although the gardener had covered the rough brickwork with climbing roses and ivy. The surrounding garden bed showcased the array of ornamental and flowering shrubs. When they reached a bench, Theo told Maggie to sit, and when she did, he turned to face her.

"The other night, it was a lie when I told you I didn't feel a connection between us. From the first moment I heard you defend yourself against that cad, I wanted to know you better. But you are so lovely and full of life; I could not imagine how you would go through life without dancing or skipping. I decided it was kinder to let you find another whole man, so I flirted with those girls and said hurtful things to you, hoping you would move on."

"Why do you underestimate yourself? You saved me from the Duke, and while my feelings for you are not gratitude, I have to say I am thankful that you were sitting quietly in the corner and only showed yourself when I needed you. Your injury resulted from a conflict where you fought for your King and country, not because of a drunken escapade."

Maggie gazed unseeing into the gardens and then said, "So where do we go from here?"

"Can you forgive me? Can we recover the friendly relationship we shared? I want your permission to court you if you are willing."

Maggie shook her head, "My Father will never permit you to court me. He and my Mother think an army Captain is beneath me."

"Ah, there is something I have to tell you. When we met, I wasn't sure whether you were one of those grasping, greedy girls looking for a title and money, so when you called me Captain, I didn't correct you. I wanted you to get to know the real me, without the trappings that come with titles and wealth. Maggie, while I am Captain Theo Devine of the British army, I am also Lord Theodore Devine, Earl of Edensborough."

Maggie raised her eyebrows at his disclosure.

"In that case, please approach my Father."

Before they could talk any more, Ben appeared in the garden.

"Well, I'm pleased you two haven't killed each other, but we have important things to discuss."

Once they were seated in the sitting room, Lady Devine, who had kept Esme and Ben company, prepared to leave. Theo shook his head.

"Please don't leave, Mother. We have a tricky problem to solve, and your wise counsel may assist."

Ben began the conversation. "Maggie, the three of us decided to attend the picnic because we had committed ourselves to going. We discovered the sudden interest in Theo and your apparent condemnation of it. A mouthy Deb told us that someone had informed them that though Theo was only a Captain, he was wealthy."

Theo continued."They were most disappointed when I told them I was as poor as a church mouse; they deserted me in droves. The same person who told the girls about my wealth also spread another rumour. The rumour the gossips are circulating is that while Lord Windsor was trying to decide which sister to choose, you seduced him in the hope he would choose you."

Maggie's face had gone a deathly white, and she keened as she rocked backward and forward. Esme slid onto the settee beside her and wrapped her arms around Maggie. Ben handed Maggie a glass. "Drink this."

Maggie gulped the glass's contents, coughing and wheezing as she drank.

"Dear God, he has ruined me."

Lady Devine didn't for one moment assume the rumours to be true. "Oh, dear me, this news is dreadful."

Theo ran his hands through his hair in frustration.

"Where do we go from now? How do we fix this travesty?"

Lady Devine said, "There is no choice. Maggie must tell her family everything that has happened, not just the most recent incident but the entire harassment. This treatment goes well beyond bullying; it is persecution."

Maggie looked distraught. Her hair had escaped in its neat do, and her pasty skin gave her a deathly pallor. Her eyes, generally a sparkling blue, were dull and red rings further marred her appearance.

Theo took Maggie's hand.

"I will accompany you when you go home. Once I have your Father's permission to court you, I will remain if you wish."

Esme grinned. "What do they say about good things rising from the ashes of destruction? I will have a new sister, and that's worth celebrating."

Lady Devine hugged her son and then Maggie. "Welcome to the family, Maggie."

Maggie's tears were now those of gratitude that no one in this room believed the gossip.

Esme had a thought. "I don't believe you want Lord Windsor present when you reveal all that has gone on, so when you get home, you need to pretend to be your sister and send him a note saying you are unwell and will not be attending the event tonight. Stress that you fear you may be infectious and urge him not to visit."

Maggie nodded. "I travelled alone today, so Theo, you need to travel in your vehicle, or if you are to accompany me, I need a chaperone."

"It might be best to travel separately; otherwise, we'll have carriages going back and forth all night."

Chapter Fourteen

Despite his offer to stay, Maggie knew she had to face her family alone. Her reluctance to speak sooner had allowed the Duke to escalate his harassment to the point that she would be unmarriageable without Theo's offer to court her. When her Father arrived at the dining room, he looked pleased with himself. He laughed and said, "Who would have thought your Captain would turn out to be Lord Devine, the Earl of Edensborough? Maggie, I have permitted him to court you."

"Thank you, Father."

Layla screwed up her nose. "That soldier is an Earl? How can that be? Are you certain this isn't a ruse?"

"Layla, some men of noble birth considered it their duty to defend their country."

The meal was a tense affair; Layla's disapproval of Theo was plain to see. Maggie halted the servers as they prepared to serve the cups of tea.

"Father, I have some disturbing news to share with the family. I hoped we could take our drinks to the library."

Layla said, "Don't be dramatic, Maggie. Tell us here."

Maggie appealed to her Father. "Please, can I tell you all in private? We must have privacy."

Lord Buckingham nodded to Cummings.

"Serve the tea in the library."

A few minutes later, the family sat in the club chairs in the library, and Maggie pulled her chair around to face the others.

"Layla, what I say will upset you, but I beg you to listen. Father, do you remember when I came to you at the beginning of the season to express my concern about how the Duke monopolised us and prevented others from being our partners?"

"Yes, and I asked the man about his intentions, and he had no choice but to pick Layla, as you didn't want anything to do with the man."

"Yes, and I previously mentioned him dragging me around until Lord Reinbolt intervened."

Lady Buckingham snorted. "Maggie, are we going to rehash old stories?"

"No, Mother, we are not. I will tell you what happened between the Duke and me so you can see the type of man your daughter is engaged to. The only night I danced the waltz with the Duke was the night you found me hiding in the retiring room. The dance with the Duke began as you would expect, but as he danced, he moved us to the edge of the dance floor, where the lighting was poor. I expressed my concern and asked him to move us back to where the other dances were, and he laughed at me. He ran his hands across my bottom and squeezed my buttocks. "

"Stop, you are lying. The Duke wouldn't do that."

"He did, and he pressed me up close so I could feel his man, ah, thing pressed against my belly. Your betrothed looked down the front of my dress and commented on my breasts. He said he knew I wasn't a maiden and wanted to press me up against the brick wall out the back and tup me. The cad said he thought I would like it rough and fast."

Maggie was weeping as she recounted her ordeal; although Layla defended the Duke, Maggie's father and Mother believed her description of the events.

"No, no, you must have led him on. I've seen you flirt with gentlemen before, and maybe you gave him the impression you were open to his advances."

"Layla, be truthful to yourself. Have I ever said anything about the Duke except that his controlling and bullying ways will not make him a good husband? I have avoided him whenever I can, and you still doubt the truth of my accusations?"

Her Mother looked stunned. "When we returned that night, you asked your maid to bring a bath; was there a reason?"

"I stayed in that bath until it was cold, trying to scrub off the feeling of his hands. I felt violated and ashamed that I couldn't stop him."

Lord Buckingham's clenched fists and his colour heightened as anger rolled through him.

"Why didn't I know this?"

"I didn't tell you because I feared you might call him out, and I didn't want you to get hurt. Even if you were the victor, the reason for the duel would sweep through the ton, and although I was the victim, the ton is quick to blame the woman."

Maggie struggled to calm herself as she remembered the details of her interactions with Lord Windsor.

"As you can imagine, I did my best to avoid the man, which seemed to work until the night I met Lord Devine. I didn't have a partner for the supper dance and was tired of chit-chat. The balcony appeared empty, and I went outside for fresh air. Lord Windsor arrived and announced that Layla had sent him to dance the waltz with me, and we could eat supper together. I refused numerous times, and he kept laughing at me and saying how much he looked forward to the dance. I told him I would rather start a scandal than have him grope me again, and the cad said playing hard to get lost its appeal after a while. He grabbed my arm and began pulling me across the floor. I had thought I was alone on the balcony, but Lord Devine was sitting in a dark corner, and he intervened. Lord Windsor refused to release me until Theo produced a knife and offered to carve up the Duke's pretty face. As payback, he concocted a story about me getting a ride with someone else, and you deserted me."

Layla had stopped defending her betrothed and looked as shocked as her Mother. Despite Layla's easy acceptance of the Duke and his bullying ways, Maggie felt sad for her sister. Lord Buckingham looked haggard, and Maggie felt guilty for causing the devastated look, but she needed to tell the truth, considering the Duke's last play in this game of revenge he was playing.

"Why tell us this now, Maggie?"

"Because the Duke has put his last attempt to ruin me into play. Lord Reinholt, Lord Devine, Lady Esme and I chose smaller and less prestigious affairs to attend to avoid the Duke. The first night was fun. We chatted to people. Esme and I had full dance cards, and no one turned their nose up at Ben when they realised he was a second son. However, the second occasion we went to was different. The debs swarmed over Lord Devine, and no man asked me for a dance. If I approached to chat with people, they moved away, and by the end of the evening, I was sitting along the wall like the wallflowers Ben had tried to help at the other events."

Maggie took a shuddering breath.

"The soiree we went to was worse. Ben and Esme entered together, but when Theo and I entered, several debutantes grabbed him, leaving me alone. Men sniggered, and ladies whispered behind their fans, so I hid in the retiring room. At one stage, two older ladies entered the room, called me a hussy, and said I had the nerve to attend an event with decent folk. I was confused and mortified, and after that debacle, I chose not to participate in the picnic we chose as our last event."

"Good Heavens, tell me there is no more?" her Mother whispered.

Maggie shook her head. "Sorry, but there is more. My three friends attended the picnic but left in disgust after a debutant, attempting to coerce Theo into dancing, revealed that a man had shared information with many people likely to attend our chosen events. According to the woman, the man told them that Theo was wealthy and actively searching for a wife, but he told her the information was false. Theo said he was as poor as a church mouse, and she flounced off, but not before she shared the rest of the information the man had given the group. According to the man, when the Duke was deciding between Layla and me as his wife, I seduced him to win his choice. He chose Layla because he couldn't guarantee my faithfulness."

Lord Buckingham launched from his seat, curses and oaths spewing from his mouth. Maggie had never seen her Father so angry, and when she looked up at her Mother, she realised the woman looked ready to swoon. Layla sat with slumped shoulders as the realisation that her fiancé was a monster hit her.

"I don't know how to refute his claims, and even though my friends and Lady Devine don't believe the lies, the rest of the ton does."

While Lord Buckingham ranted, Maggie's Mother rallied.

"Maggie, do you love Lord Devine? Can you see yourself happily married to the man?"

"Yes to both. Why do you ask?"

"Because, dear girl, he needs to marry you immediately, not court you."

Lord Buckingham stopped pacing as he processed his wife's suggestion.

"And Layla, sweetheart, you need never see the man again. I will break off the engagement for you and inform him that I would call him out if duels weren't illegal."

"I am so sorry, but I must discuss something related to our maids. Because I yelled at Cummings when he left me alone in the sitting room with the Duke, the servants came to me, not trusting that Mother would believe their accusations. They didn't want to be alone with the man because he had previously forced himself on two maids at his mother's house. Nobody knows if she realises this happened, and it is the reason why she can't hire young maids."

Maggie continued to relate the facts regarding the two maids and the steps she had taken to help Elsie and her family.

"It must be hard to love your child when he is the result of an assault, and even though he looks like his Father, Elsie loves him dearly."

Lady Buckingham nodded her agreement, but Lord Buckingham frowned.

"Is there no end to the man's depravity? How has his immorality gone undetected for so long?"

Maggie shrugged."He may have targeted defenceless maids before, but when you told him I didn't want him to court me, his pride was wounded, and he decided to make me pay."

"These rumours are out in public, but if I contact the magistrate, the Duke will deny his actions, and it's your word against his. We can achieve little to rectify the persecution the Duke has subjected you to, but I can let him know that I will warn any prospective brides about his depravity. The least I can do is warn other matrons that if their daughters entertain the Duke, their maids will not be safe."

Chapter Fifteen

When Theo arrived the following day, Lord Buckingham hurried him through to his office to discuss the need for a swift marriage between Maggie and him. While he didn't want to force the man into a marriage both participants might regret, he had to do all he could to protect his daughter. It was a relief to know that the idea of a speedy marriage had occurred to Theo the night before. He discussed his thoughts with his mother and sister, and as they approved, it was a matter of putting their plans into action.

"Lord Buckingham, may I have a private moment with Maggie? I don't want to force her into marrying me because she thinks it is her only option."

"In light of all that has happened, I am not adverse to you having a private word with her, but I trust you not to pressure her. She sounded receptive to the idea last night, but the revelations of the Duke's depravity upset us all. I will ask Cummings to send her in here, and I will leave."

"Before you leave, can you tell me what you intend to do about Layla's betrothal?"

"I will ask the man to call here, and I will let him know that Maggie has shared the acts of depravity he has subjected her and some other young maids to and therefore, Layla intends to break the engagement. I doubt he will accept Layla's wish never to see him again, so I will have the footmen standing by to assist me in evicting the man if necessary."

As Theo waited for Maggie's arrival, he considered all that had happened for him to get to this point. Despite the horrid things the Duke had done, Theo had no intention of marrying Maggie if she wanted to wait. While the ton forgot the rumours and moved on to gossip about someone else, a vacation in the country might be necessary if Maggie wished to postpone their marriage.

When the door opened, his heart almost stopped at seeing the previously bubbly, happy young woman as she looked now, on top of the persecution the Duke had subjected Maggie to, last night's revelation had dimmed the light in her eyes. Theo stood and held out a hand to Maggie, and when she gripped it and moved forward, he wrapped her in his arms. As Maggie wept, Theo didn't make comforting noises or banal comments; he held her tight and let her cry out her grief and frustration. When the crying jag stopped, Theo sighed and moved her from his embrace.

"I wanted our wedding to be a joyous event, a celebration of our lives and a commitment to a life together. Thanks to the Duke, it will be a quiet affair attended by our closest friends, family, and devoted servants. But my commitment to you is strong. Do you wish to marry now or retreat to the country to lick your wounds and marry later in the year?"

Maggie gave a wan smile. "Is that a proposal, my Lord?"

Theo grinned and clasped her hands. "Getting down on one knee is possible, but raising myself is messy, so I will forgo that part of the proposal. Maggie, my love, the first day I met you, even though I couldn't see your face, I was proud of how you rejected the Duke. When you turned around and saw the light in your eyes and beautiful face, I knew my heart was yours. Maggie Buckingham, will you do me the honour of becoming my wife?"

Maggie nodded. "Yes, yes, I will."

"So, is it to be a quick wedding, or do you want to return to the country and marry later?"

"I think a quick wedding might be the way to go. If I wait too long, you might change your mind."

Theo laughed. "That won't happen. Maggie, your Father will return soon, so I have to ask this: may I kiss you?"

Maggie stepped towards Theo. "I'm not sure what to do; I have never kissed before except on the cheek. Please tell me you won't kiss me on the cheek."

Theo growled. "Not a chance. Come here, and I'll show you what to do."

Theo cupped Maggie's face and lowered his mouth to hers. The kiss was whisper-soft, and Maggie sighed. When Theo pressed his mouth more firmly against hers, Maggie felt tingling along her spine and thought she would enjoy her marriage to this honourable and considerate man.

Theo's voice was gruff as he said, "Your Father trusted me to be a gentleman, so more kissing may have to wait. Come, we will tell your family of our decision."

Despite the speed at which she had to organise the wedding, Lady Buckingham was excited. When the season began, she never thought that a marriage would result from Maggie's infatuation with a man they all thought was an army officer. Lady Buckingham watched the interaction between her daughter and Lord Devine and realised that she had nearly subjected Layla to a loveless union. The affection between Maggie and the Earl was a joy to see, and Lady Buckingham vowed to make the wedding ceremony a special occasion.

Because of the Duke's vindictiveness, the wedding needed to be within a few weeks, and although Maggie was excited at her upcoming nuptials, she was sad that the wedding she dreamed of as a girl would not eventuate. With Theo as her husband for a lifetime, Maggie pushed aside her disappointment and helped her mother with the arrangements.

Layla's distress and heartbreak were the one thing that dampened the upcoming celebrations. Maggie knew that Layla was better off without the man and that while Layla's distress was tangible, the person she grieved for was fictional. After being swayed by his title and wealth, Layla had built the Duke into a fictional hero who didn't exist.

Lord Buckingham confronted the Duke about his treatment of Maggie and ended the Duke's engagement to Layla. While the man tried to bluster his way through an explanation of his treatment of Maggie, he received the termination of the betrothal with rage and threats of violence. Lord Buckingham was concerned that the man might carry out his threats, but the only course of action was to move forward and keep his family safe. After a discussion with Theo, Lord Buckingham hired ex-soldiers known to Theo to protect the ladies of his family. As an added safety measure, Lord Buckingham and Lord Devine visited the magistrate to express their concerns regarding his volatile nature and the dangerous threats made to the family. If Lord Windsor attempted to harm his family, he wanted the magistrate to be aware of their concerns.

Chapter Sixteen

Maggie's wedding went off without a hitch, and the only unhappy face belonged to Layla. After lengthy discussions, the family decided to leave for the country until the gossip died. While Maggie would miss her family, she was eager to start her new life with Theo. Concerned about the Duke's threats, Theo told his mother and Esme they would be safer in the country. Esme and Ben's romance had led to their courtship, and, not wanting to be separated, Esme convinced Ben to join them in the country.

With the family in attendance, Maggie fretted about her wedding night. Would she dislike Theo's attention as much as she hated what the Duke did? Without her Mother present, she felt she had no one to talk to until Lady Devine asked her to stroll through the gardens together. As they walked, Lady Devine pointed to particular shrubs and plants and with her mind distracted by the upcoming night, Maggie understood very little of what Theo's Mother told her. When they reached a bench, Lady Devine said they should sit and took Maggie's hand.

"Maggie, after your interactions with that debauched Duke, I can tell you are concerned about what will happen tonight."

Maggie shuddered. "I felt violated and dirty after the Duke groped me, and my Mother told me so little of what happens in the marriage bed that I am concerned. What if I find Theo's attentions as repulsive as the Duke's?"

Lady Devine patted the hand she held. "Maggie, the things Theo does tonight will be done with love. The wedding bed may be a trifle embarrassing at first, but with a man you love, it becomes one of the great joys of marriage. If your Mother told you, as many women do, to lie still, close your eyes and open your legs, she has missed a lifetime of passion. Men take mistresses because their wives make it clear that they don't enjoy intimacy, and the need to beget an heir is the only reason they submit to their husbands' advances. Most men have the skill to satisfy a woman, which is why women become mistresses. They wouldn't agree to be a mistress if they didn't enjoy the intimacy. If Theo does anything you don't like, tell him. His sole interest will be satisfying you, so try not to be shy."

During this conversation, Maggie's face blazed a bright red, but she considered her Mother-in-law's words. What she described sounded far more appealing than her Mother's brief explanation.

"Thank you for explaining things to me. I know Theo loves me and would do nothing to hurt me, but your explanation helps settle me."

When Theo decided it was time to retire, Maggie couldn't control the blush that had bloomed across her cheeks. Everyone knew what they were going to do, and the thought unsettled her. Theo had dismissed her maid, and with a wink at his new wife, he said he would act as her lady's maid tonight. Theo wasn't insensitive, but a conversation with his Mother about Maggie's nervousness stayed with him.

"Maggie, I know you must be remembering that debauched cad groping you, but tonight, I want to replace that memory with pleasant ones. If I go too fast or do something you don't like, please let me know. Our intimacy tonight is supposed to be pleasant for you, so let me know if you feel uncomfortable."

Maggie laughed. "You haven't done anything yet, and I feel uncomfortable. With the mothers and dowagers of the ton forbidding even a peck on the cheek between couples, it's no wonder so many men support mistresses. By the time the women of the ton finish brainwashing girls, the chance of relaxing into a man's ministrations becomes almost impossible. I promise to try to enjoy what you do; I love you and don't want to send you into another woman's arms to seek relief or enjoyment."

"Come here, sweetheart."

Theo unlaced her dress and stayed, turning her around so he could see her face. As her dress and stays slipped off her, she was left in only her chemise. When Theo untied her braid and ran his fingers through her hair, Maggie waited for what would come next.

"Take off my shirt, Maggie."

Maggie's fingers fumbled with the buttons on Theo's shirt, and as much as he wanted to help her, he knew she needed some control. Maggie parted the shirt and gasped at his torso. His chest muscles were solid and covered in a light sprinkling of dark hair. Maggie had never seen a man in partial undress, and she felt bold as she slid the shirt from his torso. Even though a blush stained her cheeks, she drank in the sight of his naked chest. Reaching out tentatively, Maggie ran her hands down Theo's chest. He growled at her touch and pulled her towards him for a kiss. The kiss they shared after his proposal was tame compared to this kiss; Maggie's senses felt scrambled, and her heart rate increased. The feel of his lips on hers made Maggie groan, and when Theo moved from her mouth to her neck, she felt like she might swoon.

Maggie was thrilled with every new exploration of Theo's hands and mouth. He encouraged her to touch him, and as her hands skimmed over his taut back, she marvelled at how firm his body was. When his mouth moved to her breasts, she felt a moment of concern, but the swirl of his tongue over her nipples and the suck of his mouth distracted her completely. She squirmed against Theo, trying to ease the ache she felt between her legs.

"Maggie, I can ease the ache, but you must trust me. Will you let me help?"

Maggie moaned. "Yes."

"Open your legs."

Ah, this is what her Mother told her about.

"Do you want me to close my eyes and lie still?"

"Damnation, it always amazes me when other husbands tell me what their mothers-in-law tell their brides. No, I do not want you to close your eyes, and you can squirm as much as you like. We are supposed to both enjoy this, and you lying still and closing your eyes will make neither of us happy."

The touch of his hand made Maggie jump, but as he moved it over her wet centre, she sighed. Theo's touch was firm but gentle, and he found a place that made her squirm even more.

"Theo, you said this would help the ache. All you've done is increase it."

Theo chuckled. "Give me a minute, and I promise it will help."

When her orgasm hit, Maggie screamed his name, and Theo smiled with satisfaction. His little maiden was responsive, but he knew the next part might hurt. When Maggie came down from the high her orgasm caused, Theo said, "This next part might be uncomfortable, but if you relax, it will be better."

As Theo coated his engorged erection in her juices, she hummed at the exquisite feeling. Her contentment disappeared as Theo tried to breach her centre, and she clenched her muscles in response.

"Sweetheart, relax your muscles. I promise this feeling will be as good for you as it is for me if you relax. "

Maggie took a few deep breaths and willed herself to unclench her muscles. As Theo pushed inside, Maggie felt full, which was weird as she had never thought of herself as empty. She had begun to enjoy the sensation when Theo said, "Sorry, my love", as he thrust hard.

Maggie screamed. "Stop, stop, it hurts."

Despite his desperate need to move, Theo lay still, and when he felt Maggie's muscles relax, he said, "Are you right now?"

"Hmm."

Theo felt Maggie move slowly, and when she seemed to like the sensation, he breathed a sigh of relief and started to move.

"Wrap your legs around me, Mags."

Later, when Maggie snuggled into Theo's arms to sleep, she felt boneless and at peace. Her last fleeting thought before she drifted off was sadness that he Mother had never experienced the same passion that she had.

Chapter Seventeen

Time in the country moved slowly, but Maggie wasn't in any hurry to return to the city. All that awaited her were whispers about her supposed past and why she would want to trade her serenity for the madness of high society; it was anyone's guess. Unfortunately, Maggie knew they would have to eventually return because Layla deserved her support for the upcoming season. Thinking about the season brought reminders of the Duke, and she would prefer never to think of the man again. Letters from her Mother mentioned that after the argument with her father, the Duke had kept a low profile. There were unanswered questions about Layla's broken engagement, which made some Mothers cautious about the man.

Esme and Ben became engaged, which was another reason to return to the city. Maggie looked forward to helping Esme with her trousseau, something she missed when she married Theo in haste. Appointments at the top modiste had to be made well in advance, and Esme had secured appointments in a month. While Maggie looked forward to helping Esme and Layla choose new gowns, she felt confident that the old bidddies who were so quick to condemn her would still be looking for reasons to criticise.

The door opening interrupted her thoughts, and she turned to find her good-looking husband standing there. Maggie smiled at the man; he was everything she could want in a husband. He was handsome, but he also had a sense of honour, integrity, and a sense of humour.

"What were you thinking about that put that frown on your face?"

" I was thinking about returning to the city. I know we must because Layla deserves some support after last season's disaster, and of course, I need to help Esme choose her trousseau."

Theo slid an arm around her waist and drew her towards himself.

"Do you regret not having the time to choose garments for your trousseau?"

"Yes, I do. Ever since I was a little girl, I wanted the frilly white dress for my wedding and a big cake and the time to choose garments for my trousseau, but the truth is, after what happened with the Duke, I was glad you still wanted me, and I needed your love to help me heal. I have felt content and at peace here on your lovely estate, and God willing, it's a beautiful place for our children to grow."

"It's our estate, my love, not mine. But that reminds me; when we go to the city, I must make arrangements for you if I die before you do. I won't leave you penniless and at the mercy of some other man."

"Thank you for thinking of that, but don't talk about dying. We've only just found our happiness; surely God couldn't be so cruel to take you away from me."

The time to return to the city arrived, and while Esme was excited to begin the preparations for her wedding, Maggie was sad to leave her sanctuary. The two-day journey was long and arduous, broken by short stops as the driver and footmen changed the horses. Maggie hated carriage travel, and the nights spent in the inn's accommodations were a trial in themselves. Even the best inns had noisy patrons and the ever-present stench of alcohol and cigars.

When they reached the city outskirts, Maggie held her handkerchief to her nose to subdue the stench of the dilapidated homes that housed thousands of people in close quarters. As they moved further into the wealthy suburbs, the smell disappeared, and Maggie wondered what it would be like to be poor, living in squalid conditions. A wave of sympathy swamped her, and she turned her face to snuggle into Theo's warm chest.

The family settled into city life without much difficulty. Even though the Duke had kept a low profile, Theo contacted the friends who had acted as guards at the end of the last season, and the men resumed their duties. After what Maggie had suffered at the hands of the Duke and then the gossip-mongers of the ton, Theo was taking no chances with her safety.

Despite Maggie's reluctance to return to the city, she enjoyed shopping expeditions with Layla and Esme. While Layla needed to update her wardrobe for the upcoming season, Esme was in the midst of complete wedding preparations, and her dress for the special day was her top priority. Maggie added three dresses to her wardrobe, but since she and Theo didn't plan to attend many functions, she didn't need to replace her wardrobe. Additionally, Maggie had suspicions that she might be pregnant; if so, her dresses would need to be restyled. Even though Maggie was excited, she kept the news to herself until she was sure there could be no mistake. She needed a doctor to confirm her pregnancy, but asking him to make a house call was equivalent to making a full-scale announcement. Confirmation could come after she missed her second monthly courses, but keeping her suspected pregnancy secret became more challenging as tiredness slammed into her. She had a suspicion Lady Devine knew the truth, but the lady was discreet and not given to gossip, so if she suspected that Maggie was with child, she would keep her suspicion to herself.

Layla didn't feel up to keeping Esme company on today's excursion to purchase clothes for her trousseau, so Maggie and Esme headed out without her. By the time they had ordered the special garments that Esme wanted, Maggie felt the strain. As the women left the shop, Maggie sighed; sitting would be a relief. Jack, their bodyguard, lowered the carriage steps and assisted Esme in boarding the vehicle, but then everything went wild. A gunshot sounded, and a second shot rang out before Jack could draw his gun. Rough hands grabbed Maggie, and Esme reached for her as she struggled.

"Sit down and shut up, lady, or I'll shoot you too."

The kidnapper threw her over his shoulder and jogged to where an old, handsome cab waited. The man bundled her in, and the cab took off at breakneck speed. Before Maggie could scream or call for help, the man gagged her and tied her hands behind her back.

"Now, just behave yourself; the cove wants you undamaged, and I intend to collect the large payment he promised for your capture."

Maggie lay on the dirty floor of the old vehicle, trying to make sense of this kidnapping. Did some rogue intend to hold her for ransom? Fear for herself and her unborn child welled, and she wept. The carriage seemed to drive for ages before pulling into a quiet street. When the thug pulled her from the carriage, Maggie looked around in despair. This area was one where people minded their own business and would look away should she call for help. As one man pushed her towards a derelict building, the other took off in the cab. Was she to be left at this thug's mercy?

When the man unlocked the outer door of the building, he pushed her into a cavernous space with a few basic cooking utensils and nothing else. The man grabbed her arm and pulled her towards another door, and while she looked around for a means to escape, he unlocked the door and pushed her inside. '

"Welcome to your new cosy quarters. I'm sure you will be delighted with your lodgings."

He slammed the door with a cackle, and she heard the bolt slide home. She was trussed up, gagged and abandoned in this filthy room. A putrid-looking bed and a chamber pot were the only pieces of furniture in the room. With despair, she looked around the room. Her only avenues of escape were the bolted door or the barred window. She looked out the window, but no person was in sight. How long would the unknown assailant keep her hostage? Did Theo know she was missing? Without the answers she needed, Maggie wept.

Chapter Eighteen

While the thugs raced away with Maggie, Esme was traumatised but coherent enough to know that the driver and Jack needed medical attention, and her brother and his friends needed to look for Maggie. With Jack lying on a seat in the carriage, Esme sat with the driver, fearing that he would pass out and kill them all. She was relieved when the man cautiously steered the vehicle into the driveway, and once the carriage came to a stop, she ran towards the front door. Cummings, who had heard the carriage pull up, opened the door as Esme raced inside.

"Cummings, we need a doctor for the driver, Jack, Bow Street runners, and the magistrate. Where is my brother?"

Theo heard his sister's commotion and entered the hallway to see what the fuss was about. One look at Esme's distraught face killed the joke he was about to make.

"Theo, they shot the driver and Jack and kidnapped Maggie. A thug grabbed her as we entered the carriage. I saw the hackney they escaped in, but it was old, and the horses were none too flash."

Theo pulled his sister into his arms for a hug and said to Cummings, "Has someone gone for the doctor and the police?"

The usually stalwart servant looked less than calm at the tragic circumstances, but nodded to indicate that he had set the requests Esme shouted at him into motion as she entered the house. Esme was still weeping, and with shuddering sobs, she said, "What do we do now?"

"If the runners and the magistrate arrive quickly, we can set up a search, but I will call in my army buddies to help. We'll search every corner of this god-awful town until I find her. Esme, please find Ben and Cummings; please send the police to the library when they arrive. Please check on the driver and Jack and let me know how they are doing."

Theo poured himself a stiff drink and cursed the assailant who kidnapped his wife. He didn't blame Jack for the kidnapping; his presence gave the ladies the confidence to go out in public and was supposed to deter the Duke of Berwick. Even with no ransom note, Theo was almost sure that Maggie's kidnapping was the Duke's revenge for ruining his reputation, and when he found the man, he would mete out the punishment he deserved.

The sound of voices outside the door heralded the arrival of Ben and the Bow Street runners. Esme repeated her account of the kidnapping, and the runners asked questions.

"Did they say anything about what they were doing?"

"He said if I tried to help, he would shoot me, too. He told Maggie to behave herself because the cove who hired him wanted her undamaged, and the thug said he wanted the hefty payment for delivering her."

Theo and Ben looked at each other.

"Men, we are looking for Lord Frederick Windsor, the Duke of Berwick. He had an obsessive interest in Maggie before we married, and I believe this is his work."

Once they drew up a plan, the groups headed off to search for the Duke and any buildings he might own, hoping to discover Maggie's whereabouts. Esme could do little but wait as the men trolled the areas where Maggie might be. While she waited for the men to return, Esme mulled over when she would start if she were organising the search. When they returned that night, Esme fretted, the idea firmly planted in her mind. Theo pushed his dinner plate away and stood. Before he could leave the room, Esme said, "Theo, I have a suggestion about the search."

"Esme, I know you are trying to help, but we are doing everything possible."

As Theo turned to leave, Esme raised her voice. "You are not doing all you can, and if you don't hear my suggestion, tomorrow, I will go and search for myself."

Theo returned to the table. "I am here; tell me your suggestion. Ben and I need to retire to bed because we have a long day ahead."

"From where I've been sitting all day, you missed one vital point. To find the thugs, you need to find the hackney. Why not assign some of your runners or soldiers to investigate places that hire old carriages? The horses were both in poor condition, and the carriage was old, so you needn't check the reputable sites; just carriages that ordinary folk would hire.

Another consideration is that if you are hunting in the city's slums or impoverished areas, you should offer a reward. Pay anyone who notices something unusual in the buildings around them or where they travel daily."

Ben cocked his head. "Good thinking, sweetheart, but what kind of thing would we reward?"

"You'd pay for information like, has anyone seen a man fitting the Duke's description in the less affluent areas, or a building that nobody uses that suddenly seems to have a lot of activity?"

Theo rose from his chair. "Thanks, Esme; I have been so worried, I fear my brain isn't working well. Your suggestions are good, so if you come up with any others, we will listen."

Theo was more in command of his brain when the men gathered the following day. He knew he needed to keep a clear head if they had any hope of rescuing Maggie. The Bow Street runners began to trawl the city for carriage hire, and the remainder of the men split into two groups. The soldiers, dressed in poor-quality clothing, could blend in with the crowds that thronged the streets. At the same time, Theo, Ben, and two other friends rode through the streets, offering a reward for information that would lead to Maggie's rescue.

As they rode the streets, thoughts of Maggie plagued Theo. Was she hurt? Did she know he would do everything possible to rescue her? It was hard to believe that the Duke was so deranged as to wait four months before seeking revenge.

Chapter Nineteen

Maggie

As night fell, Maggie slumped against the wall behind the bedhead. While the thought of the bugs and filth in the mattress made her cringe, Maggie decided that the bed was a better option than the floor, which was crawling with rodents and insects. Her arms ached from the unnatural position tied behind her back, and she needed to use the privy, but the situation could be messy without using her hands to tuck up her dress.

Footsteps on the staircase outside her room made her stomach clench. Was the person who wanted her kidnapped showing himself, or were the thugs coming back? Tucked tightly against the wall, Maggie watched with dread as she heard the lock disengage and the door swing open. When the Duke entered the room, she looked with horror at the man who had caused her so much grief during her first season.

"You! You despicable cad. Why am I held captive? Let me go at once."

Lord Windsor chuckled. "You, my dear, are in no position to make demands. I will release you in a few months when you are well used and growing fat with my babe in your belly. Let's see if the soldier still wants you then."

Maggie's mouth fell open in horror. With a babe in her belly already, the Duke couldn't make that part of his revenge come true, but would Theo want her if she were used frequently and then thrown out by this cad?

Lord Windsor could see the fear on her face and laughed.

"Let's see if your husband is an honourable man or if he will divorce you for the trollop you are. Once I'm done, you might have the skills to work at one of the bawdy houses, or if you're lucky, some old codger will take you as his mistress."

"Are you going to untie my hands? I need to use the privy, and I'm sure you will not want to touch me if I wee and defecate all over myself."

"I will untie you, but if you dirty yourself to prevent me from taking my pleasure, I will throw a bucket of water at you to clean you down."

Maggie turned her back for the man to untie her hands and shuddered in disgust when his hands ran across her shoulders and into the cleavage of the dress. Twisting wildly, she attempted to evade the man's hands, but with a sharp twist, he made her cry out in pain as he bent her hands backward. When Maggie's hands shot free of their binds, she groaned. Pins and needles shot through her arms and shoulders while her abused hands stung from the Duke's treatment.

"Ah, Maggie, this could have been so simple. If you had been compliant, I could have married your sister and kept you as my mistress. I don't have the pleasure of torturing your innocent little sister, but I will bed you. And the best part is, you will beg me to take you when the hunger pains get too bad, and I will feed you if you please me in bed."

"Don't get too tired waiting. I would rather die of starvation than have you bed me."

The Duke laughed and strode from the room without a backward glance. Once Maggie was sure the evil man had left, she used the privy and then looked around the room. The window was the only possible escape route, but the bars attached to the sill made this option impossible. When footsteps sounded outside her door, Maggie braced for the entrance of the Duke, but much to her surprise, a woman entered the room. The woman carried a hunk of bread and a skin of water, which she placed on the floor near Maggie.

"Back away if you want the food before the bugs eat it."

Maggie stepped away from the woman who put down another chamber pot and disappeared with the soiled privy.

"Please, if you help me escape, my husband will pay a reward."

"The reward won't do me any good because the cove will kill me. Sorry, my lady, all I can do is bring you food."

As the woman backed away from the door, Maggie pounced on the food. The stale bread was almost inedible, so Maggie used some precious water to soften it. Exhausted by the day's stress, Maggie fell into a fitful sleep.

At the arrival of dawn, a few brave rays of sunshine struggled through the grimy windows. Maggie's prison looked no better in the weak morning light, but she stood and walked to the window; not a soul could she see, and there were no sounds of traffic or the crowded street she travelled through when her kidnappers snatched her. Her stomach rumbled, and she wondered if she would get one meal a day or two. Shortly after she inspected the room, the woman arrived with more bread and water, answering Maggie's question about how many meals she would get.

As she attempted to make her meal edible, the door opened again, and the Duke entered.

"Ah, Maggie, my sweet, it is so good to see you this morning. Did you have an enjoyable evening?"

"This place is a filthy hovel. If you had to kidnap me, you could have at least found a decent place to imprison me."

The Duke shook his head. "Maggie, don't trick yourself into believing that you will return to your expensive lifestyle. Once I've finished with you and the soldier divorces you, this room will look like a palace. You'll be able to entertain men to make the rent and pay for food scraps."

Maggie hung her head, unwilling to let her tormentor see the terror in her eyes. No matter how much Theo said he loved her, she couldn't subject him to living with a woman who had been used and discarded. If this fiend defiled her, she would be unworthy of a place by Theo's side.

"And you look ridiculous still wearing your bonnet inside. The sun's rays won't damage your delicate skin here, and you won't see the outside of this room until I've had my fill."

The door slammed shut behind the Duke, and Maggie couldn't stop the tears. How long would he wait to force himself on her? Her one saving grace was that no matter how many times the man forced her, the child she carried was Theo's. With a sigh, Maggie pulled the pins from her bonnet and folded the garment on the bed. She slid the long hatpins into the seedy mattress and wet the bread, making it soggy enough to be edible.

Day after day, the Duke tormented her, seemingly in no hurry to defile her. The only positive thing that happened was learning of her pregnancy; the server smuggled a chunk of cheese with every meal she delivered to Maggie. Even though the woman was too frightened of the Duke to free her, she advised Maggie not to tell the Duke about the baby for her safety and the baby's safety. Gazing out the window one day, Maggie fretted about how to draw attention to her plight. The only material Maggie had in the room was the filthy covers on the bed or her bonnet. Would the bonnet be large enough to catch the eye of a passerby? Surely, a bonnet fluttering in the breeze might cause some speculation. She sensed the Duke was becoming impatient and unaware of the reason for Maggie's relatively good health. Maggie feared he would make his move soon.

After hanging her bonnet by one tie to the window's bars, Maggie looked for a weapon. As she lowered herself onto the bed, a sharp object stabbed her. With a yelp, Maggie jumped off the bed, sure that vermin had reached her bed and taken a bite of her, only to discover that the sharp object was a hatpin. Could she use it to defend herself? Maggie wasn't sure how effective the pin would be, and the Duke would need to be close to her, but she threaded it through her bodice and prayed Theo would find her before she had to put her makeshift weapon to the test.

94

Chapter Twenty

T*heo*

Theo was at a loss to discover where the Duke had hidden Maggie. His house was closed, and according to the skeleton staff, his Grace had said he was travelling on the continent. Theo and Ben didn't believe this explanation for a moment. Still, after checking the Duke's known haunts and examining vacant buildings in the immediate city area, they became frustrated by their lack of progress. The thought that haunted Theo was what Maggie would have to endure at the hands of the fiend.

Esme's suggestion to find the hackney gave them a lead, but the proprietor swore he didn't know the men who hired the vehicle, although he described them. The problem was that thousands of men in the immediate area fit the description, so they were no further advanced. With no luck in the inner city, the searchers fanned out, covering locations further from the city's heart. The sheer number of abandoned buildings staggered Theo, and he began to feel the futility of their search. He wanted to shout and cry and curse the damn Duke, but none of that would help him find Maggie.

Theo was almost ready to call off the search; Maggie might no longer be in London. The damned Duke could have transported her anywhere in the country; they were wasting their time without a clue to follow. The men gathered in Theo's library, and each was as unhappy as the others. Finishing the search didn't sit well with any of the searchers, but they didn't know what more they could do. When a tap came on the door, Theo bade the butler enter, and what the man had to say galvanised everyone in the room.

"My Lord, a man at the door says he might have information to find Lady Maggie."

"Send him in."

"Ah, milord, he's not exactly clean and tidy, if you get my meaning."

"Cummings, as long as the man is sober, I don't care about his hygiene. Send him in."

The man who followed Cummings into the room looked intimidated by the display of searchers. Theo approached the man with his hand outstretched, and the man shook it before doffing his cap to the room's other occupants.

"My butler tells me you might have information to help us locate my wife. What do you have to say?"

The man fiddled with his cap, and it took all of Theo's patience not to grab the man and shake the information out of him.

"Milord, the searchers said anything unusual might help, and I saw something this morning. The old Bell building has been vacant for years and has deteriorated into a poor state of repair. The windows always had bars, but when I was heading to my father's plot this morning, I noticed something hanging from the window. It looks like a lady's bonnet."

Theo heard the hopeful noises the men standing behind him made.

"What is your name, my good man?"

"They call me Tucker because of the bag I carry to my father's allotment."

"Well, Tucker, I will ask the butler to show you to the kitchen. Once the cook feeds you, Cummings will bring you back here to collect your reward. But if this is a hoax, I will hunt you down and cut out your tongue."

"Honest, milord, what I said is true."

"I am grateful for your information. Thank you."

After Tucker left the room, the conversations and suggestions showered down like confetti. Theo was all for setting off immediately, but Ben cautioned him.

"I am eager to remove Maggie from that fiend's control, but if we go in tonight with no plan, we might lose him in the attempt to rescue Maggie."

Theo could see sense in Ben's suggestion, but leaving Maggie in the Duke's clutches for one more night didn't sit well with him. He had to concede that if they lost the Duke in the rescue attempt, Maggie would look over her shoulder for the rest of her life.

Buoyed and excited, the searchers settled in the breakfast room at the large table and floated ideas and suggestions. The men decided to check to see if they thought it was a lady's bonnet hanging from the window, and then, if it was, they would stake out the building until they knew the Duke was inside. Their informant, Tucker, said he thought there was only one operable door on the ground floor, so Theo decided that while he and Ben rescued Maggie, the other men should search the building. Theo allocated two of the burliest men to watch the door to ensure the Duke didn't escape. With the plan made, the men settled down for the night, although Theo felt sure that at least he and Ben would sleep very little.

Chapter Twenty-One

M*aggie*

The night passed without anything untoward, but Maggie knew that the Duke would make his move come the morning. The man had spent weeks taunting her and aimed to ruin her so that even Theo would not want her. When footsteps sounded on the floor outside her door, Maggie tensed, but when the server poked her head in, left the food on a tray, and removed the privy, she sighed with relief. Maggie felt that this slight reprieve was to catch her off guard, and as she ate her soggy bread and the hunk of cheese, Maggie's fingers slid to the pin tucked securely in her bodice. With clarity, she realised that if the Duke intended to ravish her, he might start by ripping her bodice, and then she would lose the pin. Maggie's fingers trembled as she hooked the hatpin into the top of her skirt. She prayed that Theo would find her before she had to defend herself.

When the door opened, Maggie shrank against the wall and tried to appear brave. She would not cry or beg for a reprieve; the Duke might have his way with her, but he wouldn't have her self-respect.

"Well, my dear, your time to ask for mercy has arrived. If you beg nicely, I'll give you extra food after we complete our transaction."

Maggie glared at the Duke with loathing.

"I will never ask for your mercy, and if you take me, you will know that it is because you are stronger than I and not because I gave you any encouragement. You are a despicable cad, and eventually, you must face justice."

"You are so simple; I'm a Duke. No one will care if a girl makes herself available to a noble and then cries foul when her parents find out. Now, enough talk. Lie down on the bed."

Maggie shook her head, and Lord Windsor's hand lashed out and slapped her face. Maggie's head reeled backwards, but she held back the tears; her mind focused on enticing the man to get close enough to use the hatpin. When the Duke grabbed her by the arm and pushed her onto the bed, Maggie fought with everything she had. After another blow to the face, Maggie slumped on the bed, barely able to think clearly. A ripping sound pulled her from her stupor, and as cold air rushed over her bare breasts, she sobbed. Her earlier thought about him ripping her bodice had been predictable, and in her fuddled state, Maggie mourned the loss of the hatpin. As the man laughed over her bare breast, Maggie's mind cleared, and she remembered that she had the pin in her waistband. The Duke slumped over her as he reached to open the falls on his pants, and as he moved closer, Maggie held the makeshift weapon in her hand. As the man straightened, Maggie plunged the pin into his chest, and as he screamed in pain, she used her feet and shoved the man off the bed. As he writhed on the floor, Maggie searched for another weapon to use on the man, and she grabbed the privy pot and smacked him over the head with it. She hit him again for good measure, and staring at the lifeless body on the floor, she fled for the door.

As she stepped into the hallway, a firm hand grasped her arm. Maggie was hysterical with fear. She had disarmed the predator who stalked her, and suddenly another man appeared.

"Maggie, stop. It's me; it's Theo."

It took a moment for the words to make sense, and when she heard her husband's voice, Maggie slumped with relief.

"You're safe now. Where is the scoundrel who kidnapped you?"

Maggie looked over her shoulder at the door she had exited.

"He's in there, but I think I killed him. I think he's dead."

Theo looked over his wife's shoulder and raised his eyebrows at Ben. Ben motioned with his head, and Theo said, "Maggie, Ben and I need to check. Will you be alright with Jack while we look in the room?"

Maggie's breath shuddered, but she forced a smile. "Jack is alive?"

A voice she knew well said, "It takes more'n a bullet to put me out of action, milady. Let's get you covered up, and I'll help you to the carriage."

Jack draped his jacket around Maggie and led her to the waiting vehicle as Ben and Theo confirmed the Duke's death. Once they had confirmed it, the building swarmed with police and Bow Street runners. Theo spoke to the senior policeman, and then the carriage headed for home. There would be questions to answer, but at the moment, Maggie needed home comforts. Snuggled against Theo's shoulder, Maggie slept soundly for the first time in many weeks. The fear of being overrun by rats might resurface in the dark of night, but she felt safe and loved in the carriage with Theo.

Maggie's homecoming was joyous. Esme cried, and there were tears from many of the household staff who had waited anxiously for news of Maggie's return. While Mrs Beasley organised a bath, Maggie devoured the lunch the cook prepared, anticipating her return. Even though she wanted to talk to Theo, Maggie needed a bath; three weeks with no chance to freshen up had taken their toll, and with the only place to rest being a lice-ridden pallet, she was desperate to remove the crawly creatures from her hair and body. When Carrie, her lady's maid, helped Maggie to dress, she felt like a new person. Entering the sitting room, Maggie discovered that her sister-in-law, her fiancé and Theo were waiting for her.

"You can't know how good it is to be here. The place where the villain held me prisoner swarmed with vermin, and the only place to rest was a lice-infested pallet."

Esme stood and hugged Maggie. "We are so glad to have you back. I thought Theo would go mad when the searches made no progress for three weeks. I'm sure they considered giving up because there were no clues about your whereabouts, and the men began to wonder if you were still in the London area. It seemed like a hopeless task until the man saw your bonnet."

"I could hear footsteps sometimes, but by the time I reached the window, there was nobody about. I decided to hang my bonnet out the window to attract attention, and I guess it worked."

Theo leaned forward in his chair and said, "Tell me how you escaped the beast."

Maggie took a shuddering breath.

"When I tied my bonnet to the window bars, I realised I had two long hat pins. They were my only weapon, so I threaded them through the waist of my skirt and hoped the scoundrel would get close enough for me to use them. I had no grand plan, but I thought if I slowed him, I might be able to race for the door because he never locked it when he came in to taunt me. He had run out of patience today and decided to tup me. After he slapped me and ripped my bodice, he threw me onto the bed, and when I lashed out, he hit me again. As he leaned down to undo his falls, I jabbed a pin into his chest as hard as I could, and when he reared back, I kicked him and shoved him from the bed. I didn't know if the pin would stop him, so I hit him with the potty, and because he was still cursing, I hit him again. The privy pot broke, and that's when I ran for the door."

Esme shook her head. "Goodness me, you are so brave, Maggie."

Ben said, "Even if we hadn't arrived when we did, as soon as you showed your face in the areas we searched, someone would have conveyed you to us because Theo offered a rich reward for your return."

Maggie yawned. "I need to catch up on my sleep, so if you don't mind, can we leave the questions until tomorrow?"

With assistance from her maid, Maggie readied herself for bed. Before she dismissed her maid, she said, "Carrie, before you go to bed, will you light a candle and place it in the sconce here? I will be fine if Theo is with me, but if not, the night will cause me grief."

"Certainly, my Lady. I will see to that."

Chapter Twenty-Two

Theo stood in the doorway, watching his sleeping wife. What would he learn tomorrow that would cause him grief? Maggie said the Duke had lost patience, so did that mean he hadn't touched her until that morning? As Theo watched her sleep, his heart ached; was there more she wasn't telling him, fearing that his guilt might overwhelm him? Sighing, he snuffed out the candle and headed for his bed.

Theo lay still, trying to decide what had woken him. A keening noise from Maggie's bedroom roused him, and he entered her room to determine what was causing her stress. In the dark, with only a sliver of moonlight filtering into the room, he couldn't decide if Maggie was awake or asleep, but there was no mistaking what she was saying.

"Get away from me, get away, get away."

Theo touched Maggie, intending to wake her, but his touch sent her into a frenzy of shouting and screaming. Shaken by his wife's behaviour, Theo struck a match to the candle he had extinguished earlier and spoke loudly to Maggie.

"Maggie, wake up. You are safe now; wake up."

Maggie opened her eyes and shuddered after taking a moment or two to focus. Her face was flushed, and her eyes red and tear-stained, and Theo deduced that Maggie had not told the truth about how often the Duke had forced himself on her. Her words, while asleep, were clear, and he knew she was screaming for the man to leave her alone.

"Are you alright now?"

"Yes, please leave the candle lit. I can't sleep in the dark."

Theo nodded, tucked Maggie's bedclothes around her and left the room with a heavy heart.

The remainder of the night passed without incident, but when Theo heard Maggie moving around in her room early in the morning, he wondered what had woken her. Her raised voice prompted him to rise, and when his valet finished helping him to dress, he headed for the breakfast room to speak to Maggie about her anger this morning.

"Maggie, I heard you had angry words with Carrie. Is everything alright?"

Maggie looked at her husband and shook her head.

"It seems I should have been angry at you, not Carrie. Last night, when you went to bed, did you snuff out the candle burning in the sconce?"

"Yes, I did. I assumed you left the candle burning and then fell asleep. Why does that make you angry?"

"I asked Carrie to light the candle when she retired, so I didn't have to sleep in the dark. As you discovered during the night, the dark bedroom causes me grief. I will need to sleep with a candle for some time, and I'd appreciate it if you didn't snuff it out. As it appears you don't wish to sleep in the same room, it is hardly likely to interrupt your sleep."

Theo hadn't seen Maggie's temper often, but it was displayed this morning. He cleared his throat, but what could he say? She was correct; he didn't wish to sleep in the same bed until the details of her incarceration came to light. Esme entered the room, followed by Ben, so more discussion about sleeping arrangements would have to wait. They could tell from Theo and Maggie's stiff postures that all was not well, but unwilling to interfere, they took their seats at the table. After morning greetings, Theo said,

"Maggie, I've asked the doctor to attend to you today to check that there are no ongoing problems, and the magistrate will be here with the police to hear the details of the Duke's death."

As she rose from her chair, Maggie said, "Very well, please inform me when they arrive."

The others at the table watched her leave, concerned that the bright, bubbly personality they knew had been doused by her time imprisoned in the draughty hovel.

"Maggie looked happier yesterday. What happened in the night to have her so unhappy?"

"It seems I am in the bad books. Last night, Maggie asked Carrie to leave a lit candle in the sconce because she was frightened to sleep in the dark. When I checked on her, she seemed settled, so I snuffed the candle and retired. Maggie's shouts and pleas woke me, and I lit the candle before I could wake her. It was what Maggie was shouting that concerned me. She yelled, 'Get away from me,' and pleaded to be left alone. Does that sound like that beast tried to force his attention on her only once?"

Ben ran his hands through his hair, ruining his valet's attempts to confine his unruly locks.

"It does sound bad, but did you discuss what you heard with Maggie?"

"No, I'm afraid she will deny what I heard. I feel she is trying to spare me the details of what happened. She probably realises I feel guilty for not finding her sooner, and she is trying to ease my guilt."

Esme shook her head and glared at her brother.

"Have you forgotten that this mess is not all about you? You seem to expect the worst and have already backed away from supporting your wife. From what I remember of you two after the wedding, you never slept apart, but last night, when Maggie needed your support, you slunk to your bed to nurse your supposed injuries. Too bad that

Maggie needed you, and as for asking her what you heard, why didn't you ask her last night?"

The interruption from Carruthers as he announced the doctor and the magistrate was a welcome one as far as Theo was concerned. Mrs Beasley escorted the doctor to Maggie's chambers, and with her maid in attendance, the consultation was thorough. The examination confirmed what Maggie already guessed; she had asked the doctor to confirm her pregnancy, but the appointment she made was two days after the thugs kidnapped her. The doctor took his leave, and Maggie headed to the sitting room to face the magistrate, a man she had little faith in after his disregard for the village girls' complaints.

When she arrived in the parlour, the magistrate, Theo, and a policeman sat on a settee facing Maggie. She expected Theo to join her, and when he remained seated, she asked Cummings to fetch Esme and Ben. Once she had her friends placed on either side of her, Maggie looked at the officious man and said, "You may proceed with your questions."

"Lady Maggie.."

Maggie interrupted. "Sir, I have not given you leave to address me in such a familiar way. You may address me as Lady Margaret or my lady."

The man coloured slightly and said, "Lady Margaret, please tell us about your abduction."

As Maggie relayed the events leading up to her abduction, Ben placed his hand in hers, and Esme tucked her arm through Maggie's. When the man appeared ready to move on, Esme said, "Sir Gregory, I was there that day. Have you no questions for me?"

An annoyed expression crossed the man's face, but he bade Esme to add anything she could to the explanation.

"Now, Lady Margaret, tell me about your incarceration."

Maggie explained what had happened once the Duke imprisoned her. She described how the Duke believed that if he starved her, she would eventually be willing to concede to his demands in exchange for food.

"And did you?"

Maggie looked at the man with contempt. "I would rather die of starvation than agree to unwelcome advances from a man, and I find your question insulting."

"How did you survive on such small rations if you didn't trade food for favours?"

Ben interrupted. " How Maggie survived will become clear if you allow her to speak, but if you continue with your insulting questions and your sleazy innuendoes, I'll punch you so hard you'll need a week to recover."

Maggie squeezed Ben's hand. "Thank you."

"Sir Gregory, the answer to your question is much less titivating than expected. The woman who emptied the privy pot and delivered the food caught me vomiting and realised I was with child. She slipped me a hunk of cheese each time she delivered food."

No one spoke for a minute or two, absorbing Maggie's news.

"The Duke's intent, in his words, was to use me hard and often and send me back to my husband with his child in my belly. Regardless of what happened, I knew he could not return me with my stomach swollen with his child."

The magistrate frowned. "How do we know the child is Lord Devine's and not Lord Windsor's?"

"Sir, men have spent years telling women they are too stupid to do more than chat about their bonnets and ribbons. Men are supposed to be wise, but if you can't do the math regarding the baby, I suggest you also discuss ribbons and bonnets. Lord Windsor tried once to force his attentions on me, and I stabbed him as he was undoing his falls."

"The death of a leading man of society is a severe crime. I'm certain his mother will want justice for your crime."

Maggie stood, placing her hands on her hips.

"What about my justice? He abducted me, kept me imprisoned, starved me and tried to rape me. Do I not have the right to defend myself? If you pursue your vendetta against me, I will take the record of your protection of women to the highest court. Would you like to meet the maid I rescued from poverty after Lord Windsor raped her? When her father complained, you brushed his complaints aside, and the reprobate evicted the family and left them to starve in a shack in the woods. I can ask Elsie to bring her son in here; he is a replica of the cad who fathered him. Would you like me to inform the high court of the other maid that your important gentleman raped? She was lucky to have a fiancé who stood by her and married her. I am done with your questions, but I suggest you think long and hard before you blame me."

Maggie stalked out of the room, and Esme scowled at Theo.

"What say you, my esteemed brother? Will your life be easier if this pop-in-jay charges Maggie with murder? I'm disgusted."

With her hand enclosed in Ben's, Esme left the room.

Chapter Twenty-Three

Maggie lay on her bed, sobbing. Never had she thought that Theo wouldn't support her. What was that rubbish about him going mad trying to find her? That had to be a lie because since she returned home yesterday, he had done nothing but look at her from the corners of his eyes and avoid her. The kidnapping villain had not forced himself on her, but he had ruined her marriage by planting seeds of suspicion. She thought Esme and Ben supported her, but this was her husband's home —could she stay here while he asked questions that called her integrity and honesty into question?

Dinner was a quiet meal, and as the company retired to the parlour. Maggie watched Theo. He avoided eye contact with her and put on a jovial expression when talking to Esme and Ben.

"Will you be sharing my bed tonight, my Lord?"

The question was like a gunshot in the room, transfixing the others as they tried to understand why it had arisen so publicly. Theo blushed and said, "I hardly think that is an after-dinner topic, my dear."

"Maybe not, and while I hate to embarrass Esme and Ben, I want to know the answer. Would you prefer to move to the privacy of our bed chamber so we can discuss the issue?"

"Ah, I think we can discuss the issue later."

Maggie nodded, and after a short while, the awkward evening ended. Maggie sat on her bed in her room, waiting for Theo to arrive. She could hear Theo and his valet talking, and she wondered if this would become a noise she would grow accustomed to again or whether this would be the last time she would hear them.

When Theo knocked on the door and entered, he was startled to discover Maggie fully clothed.

"Are you not sleeping tonight, my dear?"

"I find it interesting that in all the time I've known you, you've never called me 'my dear.' Have things changed so much? Why do you look at me with suspicion? Can you not believe what I have said about my imprisonment?"

Theo sighed. "I believe there are things you are not telling me. Maybe it is to spare me the guilt of not being able to keep my wife safe, or maybe you would prefer to push the bad memories to the back of your mind. You say that Lord Windsor never forced himself on you, but you came back home pregnant, something you never shared with me before the abduction. You woke in the night screaming for him to leave you alone, to get off. What am I to think?"

Maggie dropped her head.

"You could think that your wife, who has never led you astray or lied to you before, has suffered at the hands of a madman and that what I tell you is the truth. But that will not happen at this point, will it?"

"Mags, I need time to process what has happened."

Maggie nodded. "I will leave for Everslea tomorrow morning. If, and when, you reconcile your doubts with my truths, you know where to find me; I will take Carrie with me. Goodnight, my Lord."

Ben and Esme stood with Theo as the coach pulled away. Ben shook his head. "I don't know what happened last night, although it doesn't take a genius to realise that you didn't share Maggie's bed. But whatever occurred, you have pushed your wife away after she suffered a horrific experience. You will live to regret your actions, my friend."

Esme dried her eyes and said, "That degenerate villain starved her, humiliated her and forced her to live in squalid conditions, and all you can say is, 'You need time.' Well, brother, all I can say is the best thing that ever happened to you just drove out the gate. Even if you decide to believe Maggie, I doubt that she will ever forgive you for not trusting her. A marriage is nothing if the couple don't trust each other. She trusted you to find her, even though she took measures to help herself. But you can't trust that what she told you is the truth."

"Berating me will not make the issue any more straightforward. What will you say when the baby looks like Windsor? Will you expect me to bring up the child while ignoring its parentage? She never told me about his nighttime visits, so the onus is on her to come clean."

"Theo, maybe she is frightened that if she tells you the man forced himself on her and the child is his, you will divorce her and cast her out of society for something that was not her fault. While I want to support you, I am a woman and know how unfair society can be. Men get away with bedding widows and bored wives, barmaids and servants, but a woman has to be pure until the marriage bed. And if there isn't blood on the sheets in the morning, the woman's virtue is questioned. Damn it, Theo. Trust her; she has always been truthful."

Theo shrugged and walked away from his sister. No one knew how he felt as he tried to accept that he might have to divorce Maggie. Never in his wildest dreams could he have imagined being in such a predicament, but unless she told him the truth, he would have to wait until the baby was born to see if she had told him the truth about the baby's heritage.

Theo heard nothing from Maggie at Everslea as the weeks passed, although he hadn't expected her to write to him. He could keep busy during daylight, but Maggie's image tortured him at night. He missed his wife's cheerful outlook, laugh and enthusiasm in their marriage bed. How was he supposed to consider divorcing her when she would haunt him forever? Sitting at his desk, he attempted to tally the week's expenditure when Cummings interrupted him.

"My Lord, Doctor Rogers is here. He says he needs to see Lady Maggie. What should I tell him?"

"Seat him in the parlour and notify Esme the doctor is here. Please ask Mrs Beasley for refreshments, and I will be there shortly."

Theo stacked the ledgers on the desktop and went to the parlour. Esme and Ben had arrived, and as he asked, Mrs Beasley had set out refreshments. The conversation was general as Theo caught up with the happenings in the town. While enjoying the break from the monotony of accounts, Theo wondered what business the doctor had with Maggie.

"Doctor Rogers, Cummings tells me you are here to see Lady Maggie. I'm intrigued. Why would you need to see my wife?"

Doctor Rogers frowned. "It is common practice for a doctor to check on his female patients as their time increases. While I may not be available to deliver Lady Maggie's baby due to having to attend to others, it is wise to gather as much information as possible so the midwife is informed. With your wife being in her fifth month, I need to check all is well."

"You are mistaken, Doctor Rogers. My wife can't be much past her second or third month."

"Lord Devine, it seems that it is you who is mistaken. Before the abduction, Carrie delivered a note asking me to visit Lady Maggie and confirm her pregnancy. I never made that confirmation because the capture occurred, but my examination showed your wife to be close to four months advanced."

"Why didn't I know about her pregnancy?"

"Lady Maggie said that after she missed her, ah, monthly, she and Carrie thought the excitement of the wedding and the move might have upset things. But when Lady Maggie missed the second time, she wanted confirmation before she told you. Lord Windsor abducted Lady Maggie before I could confirm her suspicion."

Theo shook his head, floored by the news that the baby Maggie carried was his child. "Even if that is true, I snuffed the candle she left lit in her room the night she arrived home. She woke me with her cries, repeatedly saying, "Get off me, get off." That doesn't confirm her assertion that Windsor didn't force his attention on her."

"I assume from your conversation that Lady Maggie is not here, and I can see that your failure to trust is an issue, my Lord. The day I saw Lady Maggie, she spoke of the nightmares that plagued her when she slept, if a candle wasn't left burning. Your wife, Lord Devine, was held prisoner in a filthy tenement building teeming with rats and mice. She stood on the bed in a corner at night, trying to fend off the rats and mice. During the day, the problem wasn't as severe, and she would take naps on the filthy bedding. Your wife wasn't yelling at Lord Windsor to get off the bed; she was yelling at the rats and mice."

Esme listened in horror as the doctor described Maggie's internment, and when he told how Maggie survived at night, she could no longer hold her tears at bay.

"Damn you, Theo. Didn't we tell you to ask Maggie about the nightmares? You have driven your wife away with your lack of trust and empathy."

Ben nodded. "I suggest you send for the coach and travel to Everlea as soon as possible. Maggie has always been kind and accommodating, but your behaviour on top of what she suffered at the hands of that scoundrel Windsor might be too much to forgive."

Doctor Baker said, "If there is nothing else I can help you with, I will take my leave. Should Lady Maggie return, I would happily include her in my rounds."

Epilogue

Edmonds, the butler at Everslea, opened the door for Theo with a welcoming smile.

"This is a surprise, my Lord. Is Lady Maggie expecting you?"

"No, it was an impromptu visit. Please have the footmen move my trunks to my room. Where is my wife?"

"I believe Lady Maggie is in the garden, my Lord. Would you like me to send a footman to notify her of your arrival?"

"No, thank you, Edmonds. I will stroll out to the gardens to see her."

Theo was under no illusions that Maggie would be pleased to see him. How could he have jeopardised his marriage by not asking the right questions and doubting his wife's honesty? As he exited the parlour doors into the walled garden, he saw Maggie seated at a small table, her head bent as her pencil flew. Theo moved further into the garden, and Maggie's head shot up. Her startled expression changed, and her face became expressionless.

"My Lord, what brings you here? Have you had time to think? Are you here to break the news that you will divorce me?"

Maggie's speech floored Theo. Had she guessed that he would have to divorce her if the babe was not his and she was compromised numerous times by the Duke?

"Maggie, I am here to apologise and beg for forgiveness. I have an explanation to offer regarding my actions."

"By all means, explain your actions, but while I might accept your apology, I doubt I will forgive you."

"Can you leave your sketch for the moment and return to the parlour with me?"

When they reached the parlour, Theo called for refreshments. His journey had continued well after dark, and the only time they stopped was when the horses needed to be changed and the night was too dark to proceed. Theo desperately required the refreshments but wasn't willing to delay his discussion with Maggie.

As Theo explained the misconceptions that Doctor Baker exposed, Maggie's expression barely changed.

"So you're saying Doctor Baker answered the questions you refused to ask me? How convenient."

"Maggie, I know I made a massive mistake in not asking the questions and doubting you, but in my defence, the thought that reprobate Windsor had forced you to submit made me feel ill. After your nightmare, I thought you must have decided to alleviate my guilt for not protecting you by not detailing the abuse you suffered."

"Not once, Theo, did you offer your support. When the magistrate continued insulting me, Ben told the man he would beat him if he didn't address me with respect. You sat with those men, judging me and allowing the bigot to make innuendoes about my morals."

Theo looked down at his lap. "Since we found you, my behaviour has been less than stellar, and I'm sorry. I'm sorry I let my fears overtake my good sense, and I regret not discussing your ordeal with you. Please forgive me, Maggie."

Maggie stood and looked at her husband. "I told you that I would hear your explanation, and I accept your apology, but it will take some time before I can think of forgiving you. I know, and so do you, that if Windsor had raped me and there was some doubt about the babe's parentage, you would have discarded me like a pair of ruined Hessians. The vow we took in the church should have meant that you supported me, whatever the circumstances, even to the point that you held no grudge for circumstances beyond my control. If Elsie can raise and love that little boy who is the spitting image of his father, I applaud her, but I am glad I don't have to put my mothering instincts to the test. Please excuse me, my Lord. I need to rest."

Theo watched as his wife left the room, and despair overwhelmed him. How was he to convince Maggie to forgive him? Could he live with his estranged wife until the baby was born, or would proximity to her make his melancholy worse? Theo decided to push his concerns aside until he was refreshed and better able to devise a plan.

Theo was frustrated beyond breaking point. Every morning, he and Maggie shared breakfast, but their conversation consisted of a greeting, and even when he tried to engage her, she ignored him. Theo suggested rides in the carriage, which she rejected, and he resorted to buying flowers and jewellery, but nothing seemed to thaw his wife's resentment. After an acrimonious exchange, Theo decided he couldn't live with his resentful wife. Maybe some time away might soften her resolve?

Theo's valet spent the afternoon packing his master's trunks, and when Theo retired for the night, the evidence of his failure sat against the wall in his room. Maggie had watched with dismay as her husband and his valet prepared for their trip. He would leave her again tomorrow, and Maggie wanted to shout and scream. She hadn't wanted jewels and flowers or fancy trips; all she wanted was her husband's affection, and even though he attempted to entice her with fancy baubles, he never once tried to hug her.

When Maggie heard Theo's valet leave, she unlocked the door between them and entered his room. The sight before her made her gasp; she had forgotten how sculptured her husband's chest was, and he was beautiful for a man who never appeared to indulge in physical exercise. Theo had heard the lock undo and was standing near his bed, facing Maggie as she entered.

"You are leaving?"

"Yes, I can't live like we have been recently. No matter what I try, you aren't interested, and after today's argument, I think it would be best for us to live apart."

Maggie dropped her head and then looked directly at him.

"Please don't go. I love you."

Theo's eyebrows shot up, and he remained speechless for a few seconds."Is ignoring me, refusing my gifts and shouting at me how you show love?"

Maggie shook her head. "I thought you knew me better than to believe your gifts were what I wanted. All I wanted was you. Do you know that since the carriage ride from the place where Windsor had me imprisoned, you have not touched me once? The first night, I needed you to hold me, to push away the bad dreams, but you slept in your bed, taking it upon yourself to put out the candle, leaving me in the one place I feared: the dark. You haven't hugged or touched me, and you've turned into someone I don't know."

Maggie stepped back, away from Theo.

"Not only did you not support me, you actively mistrusted me. When the magistrate made sly innuendoes and foul accusations, Ben was the one who defended me. If Doctor Baker hadn't called to see me, you would still be at home blaming me. Were you trying to decide how long to wait until you divorced me? Were you going to wait until the baby was born to see if it looked like you or the Duke? What would happen when it became clear that the baby was yours? Would you keep the child and dispose of the Mother? What was your plan?"

Maggie walked across the room and sat on the dressing chair.

"Do you remember when we met? You said I would run away when you explained why you couldn't dance. I didn't run then, and I've never felt disgust or pity at your injury. The first night we shared a bed, I couldn't decide whether to laugh or cry when you removed your wooden leg, but since then, it's become just part of our bedtime routine. I didn't strive to change you. I didn't question your explanation of where you lost your leg, and I've never asked you to explain how you lost your leg and survived such a horrific injury. I didn't push you to do things that made you uncomfortable; all I did was love you, regardless of the damage to your leg."

Theo watched with shame and dismay as Maggie's tears increased.

"Was it too much, my Lord, to expect the same from you? Your trust, your love and your understanding?"

Theo ran his hands through his hair as he looked at his wife. With her ever-expanding tummy, she was everything he wanted, and her complaints about not touching her stabbed him in the heart. Throughout this debacle that their marriage had become, the one thing he wanted to do was wrap his arms around her, but he feared she would reject him.

"It shames me to admit that everything you've said is true. I can't undo my mistakes or the hurt I caused you, but if we have a future, I promise always to support you, regardless of the situation. I missed you, but I wasn't brave enough to hug you because I thought you would reject me. After everything you've said, do you still want me to hug you?"

"More than anything else."

Theo pulled Maggie from the dressing chair and into his arms. He wrapped his arms around his wife and held her as she wept. When the tears subsided, he said, "I love you, Maggie. Regardless of what happens, I will always love you."

Maggie sighed against Theo's chest and ran her hands along his muscular back. Theo groaned when her hands circled his waist and ran over his strong arms and chest muscles. When her lips moved over his chest, Theo groaned.

"Stop, Maggie, if you aren't prepared for this to go further."

Maggie tilted her face towards his and said, "I am trying, not very successfully, it seems, to seduce you. Would you be able to help out here?"

Theo's mouth crashed over Maggie's as he feasted on his wife's lips. Despite the hurt, mistrust and suspicion, the chemistry remained unchanged. Eventually, they could restore their trust, and Theo had a lifetime to prove his faith in his wife.

When Theo's valet arrived the following day, he discovered that Theo had locked his door.

"Lord Devine, you need to rise if we are to depart after breakfast."

"There's been a change of plan. I will not be leaving. Please inform the driver."

Hamilton, Theo's valet, turned to walk away, but he encountered Maggie's maid as he walked along the hallway.

"I will make a guess and say either Lady Maggie will have locked her door, or if not, she is not in her bed."

Carrie and Hamilton exchanged looks when they heard a giggle from the main bedroom. Carrie grinned.

"Thank god, I was beginning to fear they would stay estranged for years to come. Let's leave their toilet for now. It may be quite some time before they wish to leave their bed."

Hamilton nodded. "I'm in complete agreement. It's good to know that Lord Windor's evil plan failed. The man underestimated Lady Maggie's bravery, and despite his wicked intentions, she bested him. Now they have a baby on the way and have reunited; things should settle down and provide us with a peaceful life."

Carrie laughed. "I hope so.."

Also by Robyn C Rye

Farnsworth Sisters
Marrying a Rogue
Rescuing Hannah

The Buckingham Sisters
Lady Maggie's Challenge
Layla's Unwanted Husband

The Evans Family
Sometimes Love is not Enough
Still the One
Moving Forward

Standalone
One More Chance
Lady Jayne's Reputation
Third Time's the Charm
Can't Stop Loving You

The Marriage Scam
An Unlikely Match
Searching For You
The Unexpected Suitor
The Lady and the Duke
Starting Over
An Unforgettable Stranger
The Duke's Revenge
The Temporary Wife
Against The Odds
Betrayed
No Good Turn Goes Unpunished
Lady Eloise's Soldier
Lillian's Forbidden Beau
Remember Me
Always Second Best
When One Door Closes
Coming Home to You
Chasing Shadows
Fool Me Once
Deserting Lady Audrey
My Unlikely Saviour
Lies and Deception
A New Beginning
Julia's Second Chance
The Hidden Enemy
The Maiden's Redemption
Miss Elizabeth's Season